Geronimo Stilton

PAPERCUTZ™

Geronimo Stilton

GRAPHIC NOVELS AVAILABLE FROM PAPERCUT𝐙

...ALSO AVAILABLE WHEREVER E-BOOKS ARE SOLD!

#1
"The Discovery of America"

#2
"The Secret of the Sphinx"

#3
"The Coliseum Con"

#4
"Following the Trail of Marco Polo"

#5
"The Great Ice Age"

#6
"Who Stole The Mona Lisa?"

#7
"Dinosaurs in Action"

#8
"Play It Again, Mozart!"

#9
"The Weird Book Machine"

#10
"Geronimo Stilton Saves the Olympics"

#11
"We'll Always Have Paris"

#12
"The First Samurai"

#13
"The Fastest Train in the West"

#14
"The First Mouse on the Moon"

#15
"All for Stilton, Stilton for All!"

#16
"Lights, Camera, Stilton!"

#17
"The Mystery of the Pirate Ship"

#18
"First to the Last Place on Earth"

#19
"Lost in Translation"

#1
"Operation Shufongfong"

papercutz.com

GERONIMO STILTON graphic novels are available for $9.99 each only in hardcover. Available from booksellers everywhere. You can also order online from papercutz.com. Or call 1-800-886-1223, Monday through Friday, 9 – 5 EST. MC, Visa, and AmEx accepted. To order by mail, please add $4.00 for postage and handling for first book ordered, $1.00 for each additional book and make check payable to NBM Publishing. Send to: Papercutz, 160 Broadway, Suite 700, East Wing, New York, NY 10038.

Geronimo Stilton

3 IN 1 #2

By Geronimo Stilton

PAPERCUTZ
NEW YORK

GERONIMO STILTON 3 IN 1 #2
Text by Geronimo Stilton
Illustrations by Edizioni Piemme
Geronimo Stilton names, characters and related indicia are copyright, trademark, and exclusive license of Atlantyca S.p.A.
All rights reserved. The moral right of the author has been asserted.

"Following the Trail of Marco Polo"
Original Title: Geronimo Stilton Sulle Tracce di Marco Polo
Story by Geronimo Stilton
Editorial Coordination by Patrizia Puricelli
Original Editing by Daniela Finistauri
Script by Demetrio Bargellini
Artistic Coordination by Roberta Bianchi
Artistic Assistance by Tommaso Valsecchi
Graphic Project by Michela Battaglin
Graphics by Marta Lorini
Original Cover Art and Color by Flavio Ferron
Interior Illustrations by Giuseppe Facciotto and Color by Davide Turotti

"The Great Ice Age"
Original Title: Geronimo Stilton La Grande Era Glaciale
Story by Geronimo Stilton
Editorial Coordination by Patrizia Puricelli
Original Editing by Daniela Finistauri
Script by Demetrio Bargellini
Artistic Coordination by Roberta Bianchi
Artistic Assistance by Tommaso Valsecchi
Graphic Project by Michela Battaglin
Graphics by Marta Lorini
Original Cover Art and Color by Flavio Ferron
Interior Illustrations by Wasabi! Studio and Color by Davide Turotti

"Who Stole the Mona Lisa?"
Original title: Geronimo Stilton Chi Ha Rubato la Gioconda?
Story by Geronimo Stilton
Editorial Coordination by Patrizia Puricelli
Original Editing by Daniela Finistauri
Script by Demetrio Bargellini
Artistic Coordination by Roberta Bianchi
Artistic Assistance by Tommaso Valsecchi
Graphic Project by Michela Battaglin
Graphics by Marta Lorini
Original Cover Art and Color by Flavio Ferron
Interior Illustrations by Giuseppe Facciotto and Color by Christian Aliprandi
With the collaboration of Ambrogio M. Piazzoni

Translation – Nanette McGuinness
Original Lettering and Production – Ortho
Production – Dawn Guzzo/Atomic Studios
Editorial Intern – Grant Frederick
Original Associate Editor – Michael Petranek
Assistant Managing Editor – Jeff Whitman
Jim Salicrup
Editor-in-Chief

ISBN: 978-1-5458-0159-8

Printed in China
November 2018

Papercutz books may be purchased for business or promotional use.
For information on bulk purchases, please contact Macmillan Corporate and Premium Sales Department at (800) 221-7945 x5442.

Distributed by Macmillan
First Printing

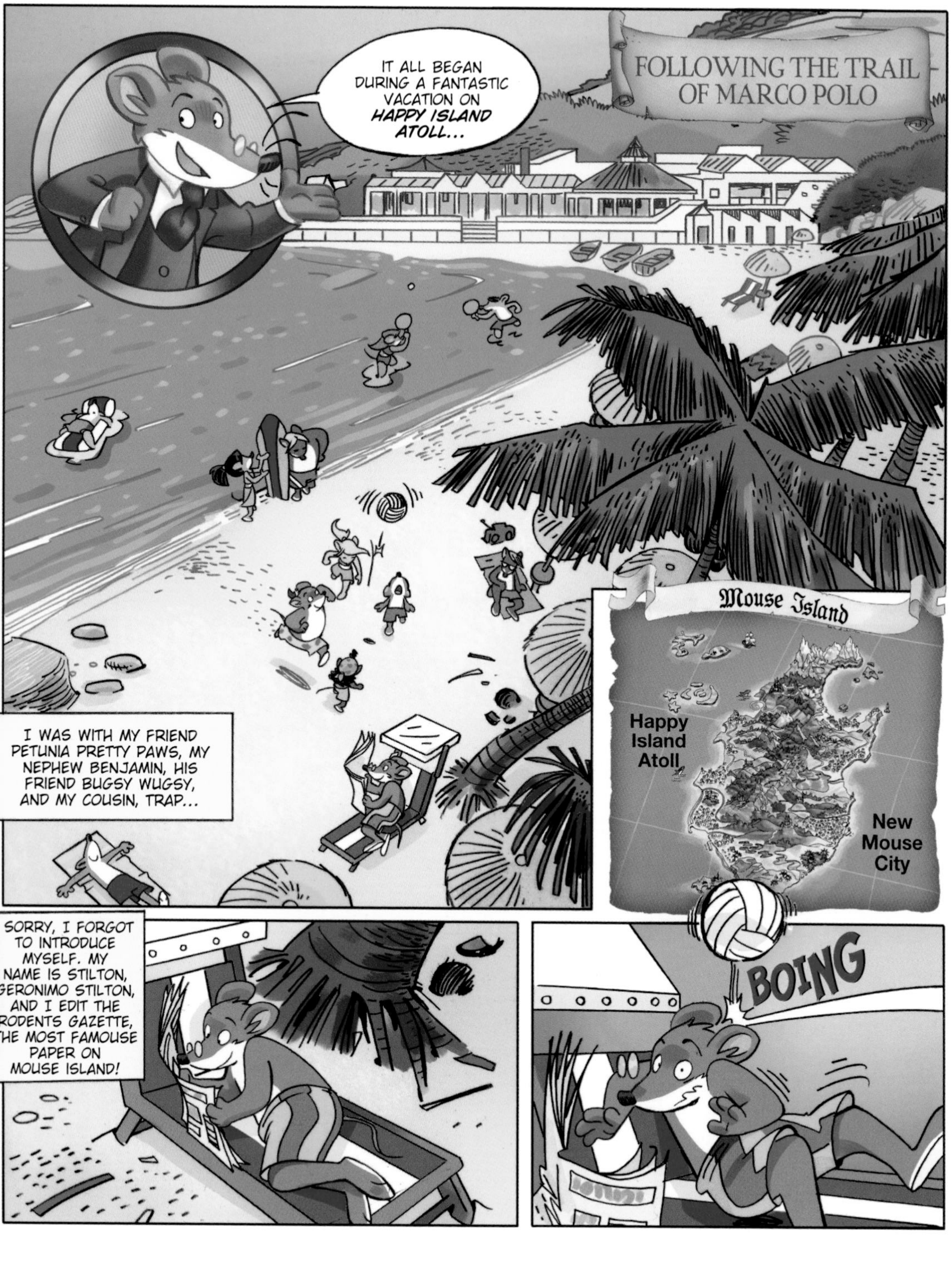
FOLLOWING THE TRAIL OF MARCO POLO
IT ALL BEGAN DURING A FANTASTIC VACATION ON HAPPY ISLAND ATOLL...
Mouse Island
Happy Island Atoll
New Mouse City
I WAS WITH MY FRIEND PETUNIA PRETTY PAWS, MY NEPHEW BENJAMIN, HIS FRIEND BUGSY WUGSY, AND MY COUSIN, TRAP...
SORRY, I FORGOT TO INTRODUCE MYSELF. MY NAME IS STILTON, GERONIMO STILTON, AND I EDIT THE RODENTS GAZETTE, THE MOST FAMOUSE PAPER ON MOUSE ISLAND!
BOING

...THEN, I WAS BLASTED BY A SANDSTORM...

I WAS ON VACATION, BUT I WASN'T RESTING VERY MUCH. AFTER I GOT HIT BY A BALL, A CRAB PINCHED ME...

...AND LAST OF ALL, I WAS MISTAKEN FOR A FISH BY A FLOCK OF SEAGULLS!

TO HELP ME RELAX, TRAP PERSUADED ME TO GO WATERSKIING...

STAND UP AS SOON THE SPEEDBOAT TAKES OFF!

UHM... I'LL TRY!

MAYBE IT WOULD'VE BEEN EASIER IF YOU'D PUT SKIS ON ME INSTEAD OF THESE THINGS!

TRUST ME, DEAR COUSIN. THOSE THINGS ARE THE AQUATIC VERSION OF SNOWBOARDS.

MAYBE SO... BUT THEY SEEM LIKE TOTALLY NORMAL BEACH TENNIS PADDLES!

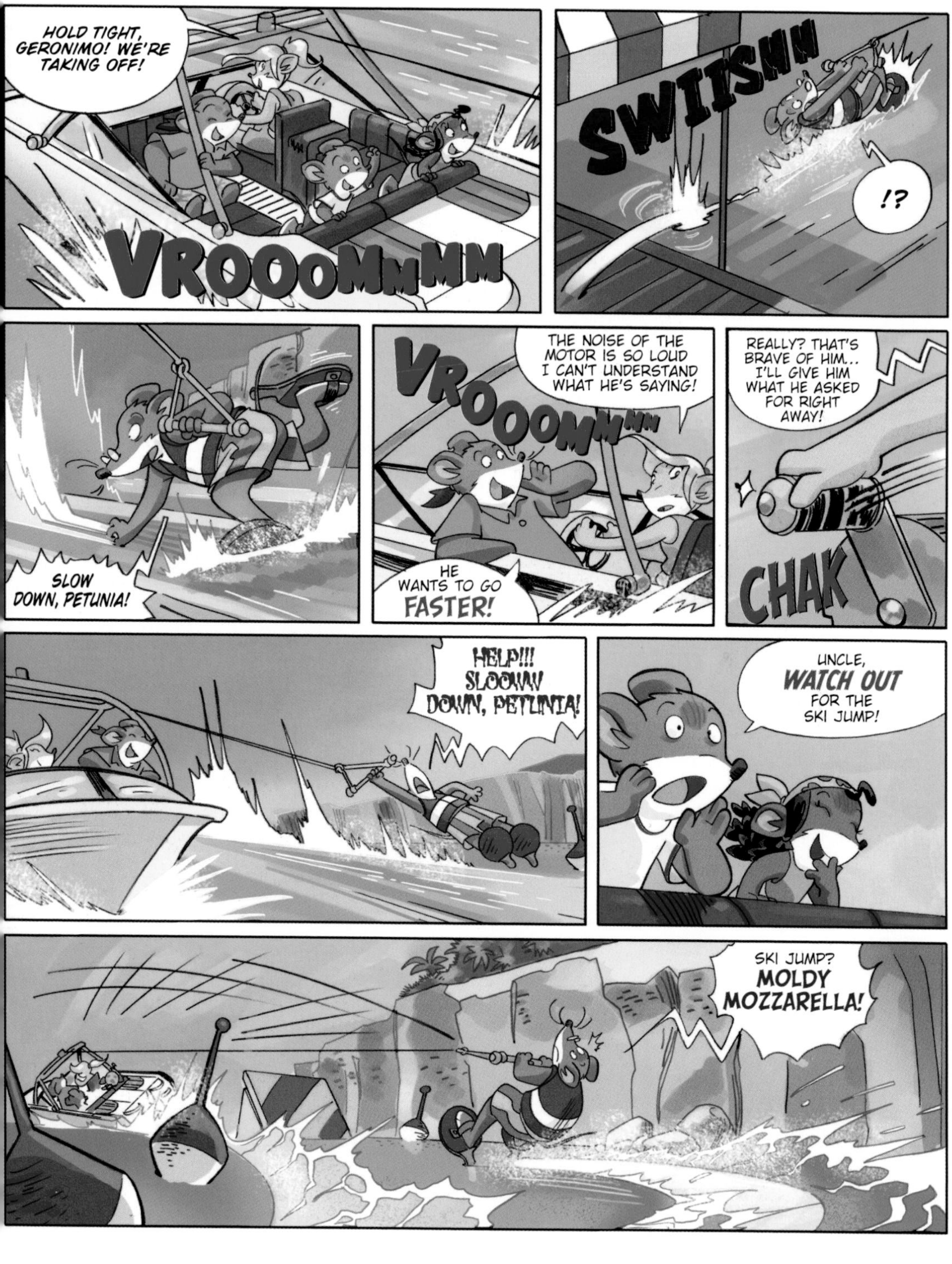
HOLD TIGHT, GERONIMO! WE'RE TAKING OFF!
VROOOMMMM
SWIISHH
!?
SLOW DOWN, PETUNIA!
VROOOMMMM
THE NOISE OF THE MOTOR IS SO LOUD I CAN'T UNDERSTAND WHAT HE'S SAYING!
HE WANTS TO GO FASTER!
REALLY? THAT'S BRAVE OF HIM... I'LL GIVE HIM WHAT HE ASKED FOR RIGHT AWAY!
CHAK
HELP!!! SLOOWW DOWN, PETUNIA!
UNCLE, WATCH OUT FOR THE SKI JUMP!
SKI JUMP? MOLDY MOZZARELLA!

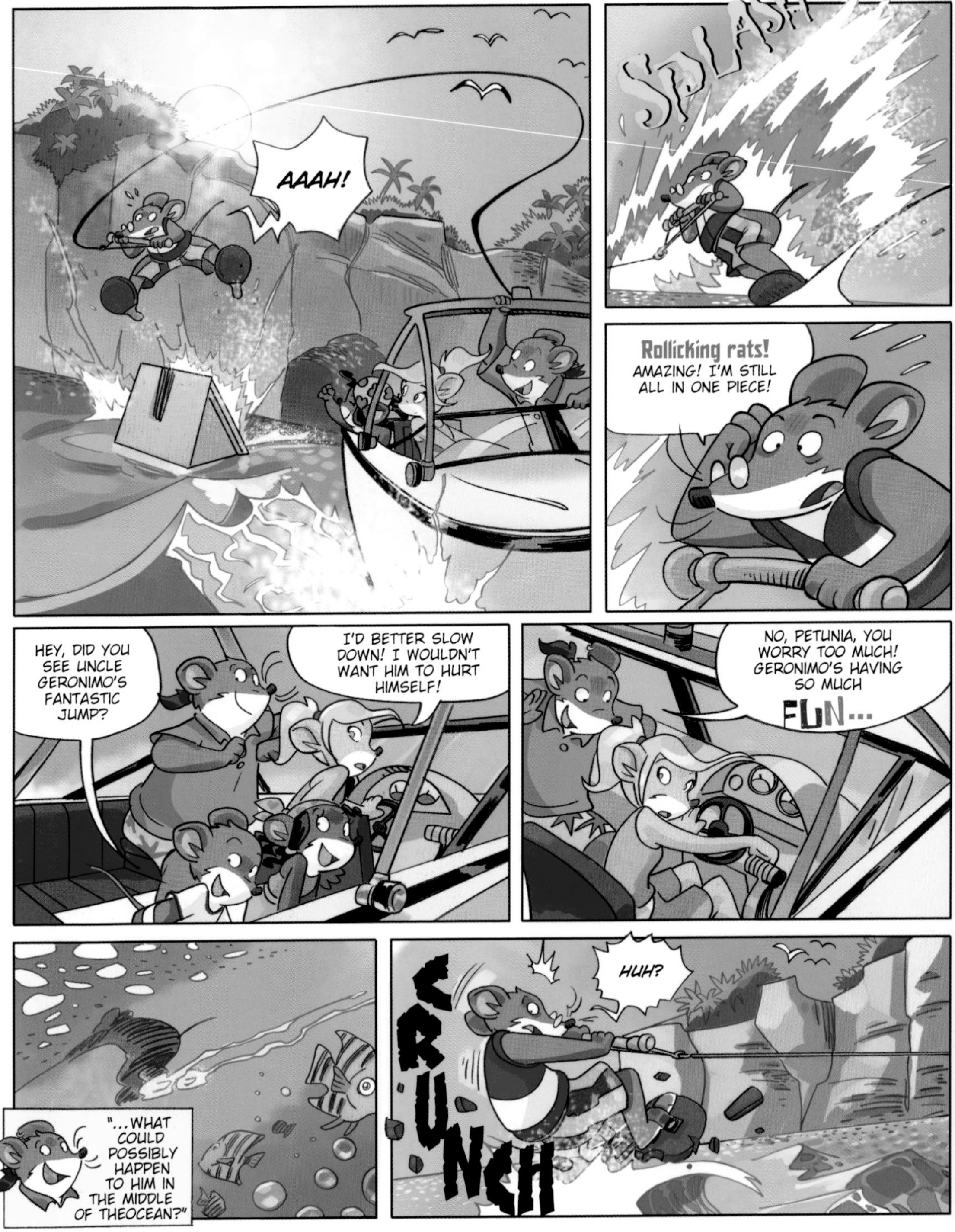
AAAH!
SPLASH
Rollicking rats! AMAZING! I'M STILL ALL IN ONE PIECE!
HEY, DID YOU SEE UNCLE GERONIMO'S FANTASTIC JUMP?
I'D BETTER SLOW DOWN! I WOULDN'T WANT HIM TO HURT HIMSELF!
NO, PETUNIA, YOU WORRY TOO MUCH! GERONIMO'S HAVING SO MUCH FUN...
"...WHAT COULD POSSIBLY HAPPEN TO HIM IN THE MIDDLE OF THEOCEAN?"
CRUNCH
HUH?

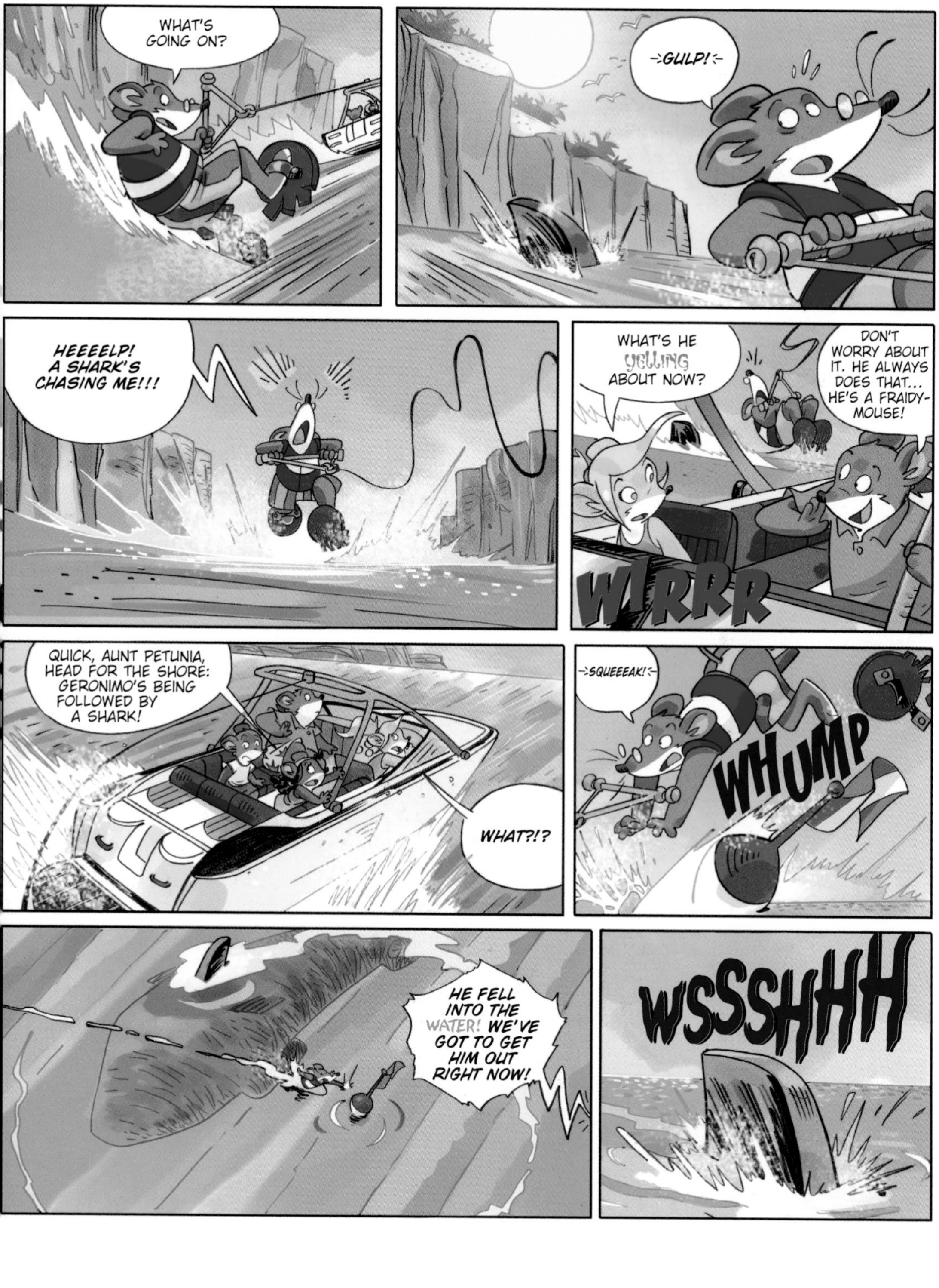

WHAT'S GOING ON?
GULP!
HEEEELP! A SHARK'S CHASING ME!!!
WHAT'S HE YELLING ABOUT NOW?
DON'T WORRY ABOUT IT. HE ALWAYS DOES THAT... HE'S A FRAIDY-MOUSE!
WIRRR
QUICK, AUNT PETUNIA, HEAD FOR THE SHORE: GERONIMO'S BEING FOLLOWED BY A SHARK!
WHAT?!?
SQUEEEAK!
WHUMP
HE FELL INTO THE WATER! WE'VE GOT TO GET HIM OUT RIGHT NOW!
WSSSHHH

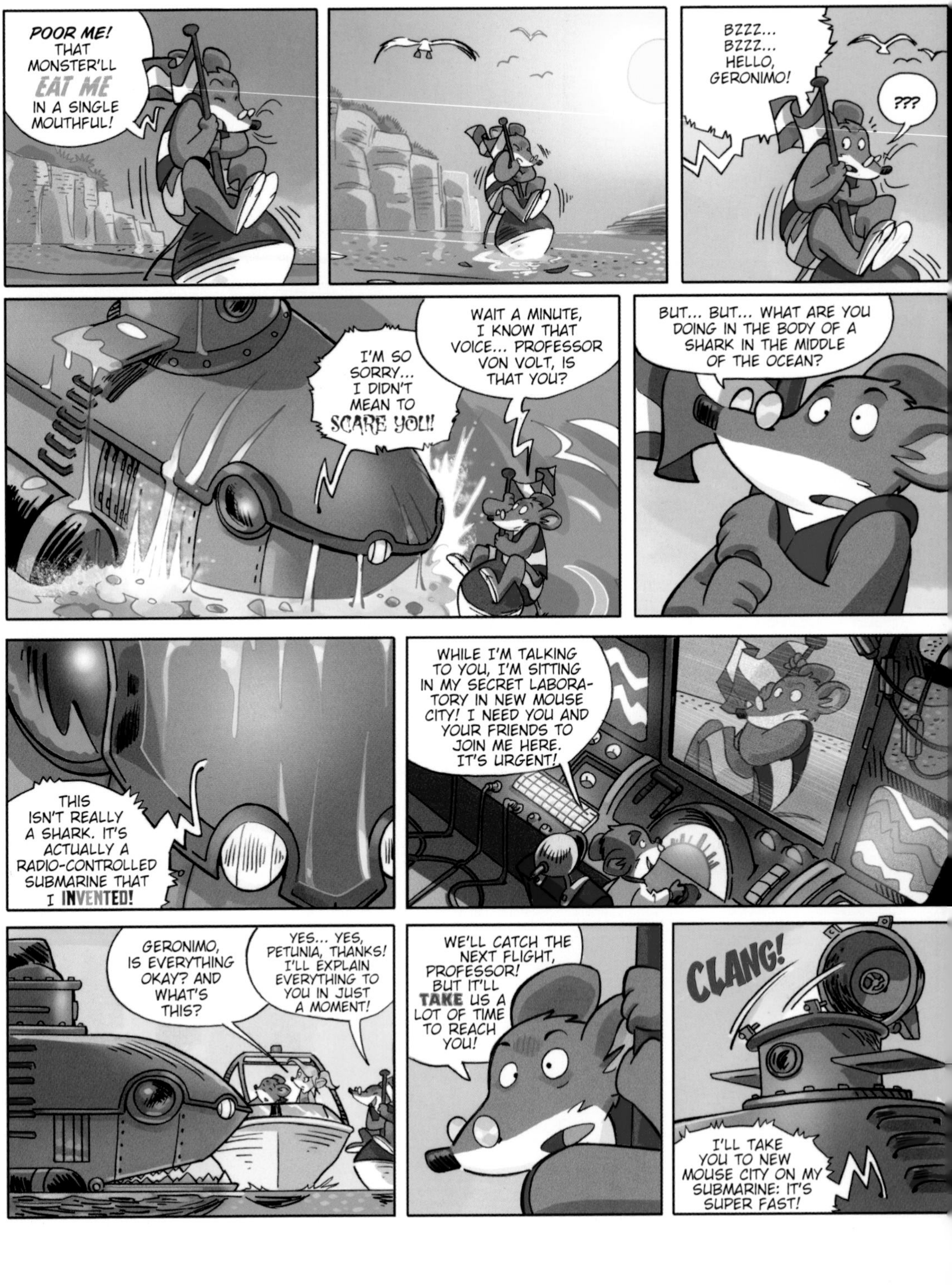
POOR ME! THAT MONSTER'LL EAT ME IN A SINGLE MOUTHFUL!
BZZZ... BZZZ... HELLO, GERONIMO!
???
I'M SO SORRY... I DIDN'T MEAN TO SCARE YOU!!
WAIT A MINUTE, I KNOW THAT VOICE... PROFESSOR VON VOLT, IS THAT YOU?
BUT... BUT... WHAT ARE YOU DOING IN THE BODY OF A SHARK IN THE MIDDLE OF THE OCEAN?
THIS ISN'T REALLY A SHARK. IT'S ACTUALLY A RADIO-CONTROLLED SUBMARINE THAT I INVENTED!
WHILE I'M TALKING TO YOU, I'M SITTING IN MY SECRET LABORATORY IN NEW MOUSE CITY! I NEED YOU AND YOUR FRIENDS TO JOIN ME HERE. IT'S URGENT!
GERONIMO, IS EVERYTHING OKAY? AND WHAT'S THIS?
YES... YES, PETUNIA, THANKS! I'LL EXPLAIN EVERYTHING TO YOU IN JUST A MOMENT!
WE'LL CATCH THE NEXT FLIGHT, PROFESSOR! BUT IT'LL TAKE US A LOT OF TIME TO REACH YOU!
CLANG!
I'LL TAKE YOU TO NEW MOUSE CITY ON MY SUBMARINE: IT'S SUPER FAST!

A LITTLE LATER, EVERYONE WAS ON BOARD...

PROFESSOR VON VOLT NEVER CEASES TO AMAZE ME!

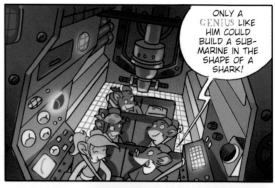

ONLY A GENIUS LIKE HIM COULD BUILD A SUBMARINE IN THE SHAPE OF A SHARK!

AND THERE'S EVEN A FRIDGE FULL OF CHEESE!

IT MUST BE SOMETHING REALLY SERIOUS IF HE CAME LOOKING FOR US WHILE WE WERE ON VACATION!

YES, YOU'RE RIGHT!

WHATEVER THE REASON HE CALLED US, WE'LL FIND OUT SOON! HERE WE ARE AT NEW MOUSE CITY HARBOR!

HEY, LOOK OUT! THE SUBMARINE IS GOING TO CRASH INTO THAT ROCK!

WHIRRR

B-BUT... THERE'S A DOOR OPENING UP IN THE ROCK UNDER THE LIGHTHOUSE!

11

IT WAS A RAT-TASTIC TRIP!

HEY! THIS TIME THE LAB IS RIGHT UNDER THE NEW MOUSE CITY LIGHT-HOUSE!

WELCOME! I HOPE YOU HAD A NICE TRIP!

WERE YOU THINKING OF BRINGING THAT FRIDGE WITH YOU, TRAP?

OF COURSE! YOU WOULDN'T WANT TO LEAVE THIS DELICIOUS CHEESE HERE!

I'M SORRY I BOTHERED YOU, BUT I DIDN'T HAVE ANY CHOICE: THE PIRATE CATS ARE BACK IN ACTION!

THE P-PIRATE CATS?

THEM AGAIN!

THE TEMPOGRAPH-- THE DEVICE I CREATED TO CHECK ON HISTORY SHOWS THEY ARE TRAVELING INTO THE PAST!

THOSE CHEESE HEADS ARE TRYING TO CHANGE HISTORY TO THEIR ADVANTAGE AGAIN!

TELL US, WHERE ARE THEY HEADED THIS TIME, PROFESSOR?

THEY'RE HEADING FOR *KHANBALIK*, THE CAPITAL OF ANCIENT *CHINA*! AND THEY CHOSE THE YEAR *1292*!

CHINA

IS A NATION IN EAST ASIA. ITS TERRITORY HAS BEEN INHABITED BY HUMANS SINCE ANTIQUITY AND HAS MANY PREHISTORIC ARCHAEOLOGICAL SITES. IT WASN'T UNTIL THE 3RD CENTURY B.C. THAT THE QIN DYNASTY UNIFIED THE DIFFERENT POPULATIONS THAT LIVED IN THE REGION AND CREATED THE FIRST CHINESE EMPIRE. CONSTRUCTION OF THE GREAT WALL BEGAN DURING THIS PERIOD. TODAY, CHINA IS ONE OF THE BIGGEST COUNTRIES IN THE WORLD: ITS SURFACE AREA IS OVER NINE MILLION SQUARE KILOMETERS AND IT HAS OVER A BILLION INHABITANTS. ITS CAPITAL IS BEIJING, WHICH WAS CALLED KHANBALIK AT THE TIME OF OUR STORY.

~SLURP!~ CHEESE! AND WHAT ARE THESE? **CHOCOLATES!**

HMM... WHY DID THEY CHOOSE THAT PLACE AND THAT TIME?

I DON'T KNOW...

...BUT AT THAT TIME, THE FAMOUS MERCHANT AND TRAVELER *MARCO POLO* COULD BE FOUND IN CHINA!

MARCO POLO (1254-1324)

WAS BORN IN VENICE, ITALY, TO A FAMILY OF MERCHANTS. IN 1271, MARCO POLO LEFT FOR CHINA WITH HIS FATHER, NICCOLO, AND HIS UNCLE MATTEO. THERE THEY STAYED AT THE COURT OF THE MONGOLIAN EMPEROR, KUBLAI KHAN, WHO ENTRUSTED THEM WITH MANY COMMISSIONS AND DIPLOMATIC MISSIONS. AFTER 17 YEARS IN CHINA, MARCO RETURNED TO VENICE IN 1292 WITH HIS FAMILY AND RELATIVES. THE TALES OF HIS JOURNEY AND HIS STAY IN CHINA ARE COLLECTED IN THE BOOK, THE TRAVELS OF MARCO POLO.

COULD MARCO POLO REALLY BE THE PIRATE CATS' TARGET?

TO FIND THAT OUT, WE'LL JUST HAVE TO **LEAVE** TOO!

A LITTLE LATER, WE WERE ON THE SPEEDRAT...

YOU'LL FIND **CLOTHES** ON BOARD SO YOU CAN DRESS LIKE A VENETIAN MERCHANT OF THAT PERIOD!

AH, I ALMOST FORGOT TO GIVE YOU MY SPECIAL EARPHONES THAT LET YOU UNDERSTAND AND SPEAK THE LOCAL LANGUAGE!

I CAN'T FIND THEM... WHERE DID I PUT THEM? I WAS SURE I LEFT THEM NEXT TO THE... CHEESE??

BY THE FLEA-RIDDEN FUR OF A WERECAT! THE CHEESE AND THE EARPHONES HAVE DISAPPEARED!

?!?

~ BURP! ~

I C-C-CAN'T BELIEVE IT! YOUR COUSIN ATE THEM!

TRAP! COULD YOU HAVE SWALLOWED SOMETHING LIKE THAT?

UMM...THEY LOOKED LIKE CHOCOLATES!

WHAT ARE WE GOING TO DO NOW? WITHOUT THE EARPHONES, WE WON'T UNDERSTAND A WORD!

HMM... LET'S SEE... LET ME THINK FOR A MOMENT...

BUT OF COURSE! I'M SUCH A NITWIT... I'LL GIVE YOU THE SPARES!

SOMETIMES THE PROFESSOR IS REALLY ABSENT-MINDED...HEE, HEE, HEE!

RIGHT! HE ALWAYS FORGETS EVERYTHING!

SO WE WERE FINALLY READY TO GO...

ZZZOOOOOM

BREAK A PAW,✱ FRIENDS! THE PRESENT AND THE *FUTURE* ARE IN YOUR HANDS!

✱ GOOD LUCK

14

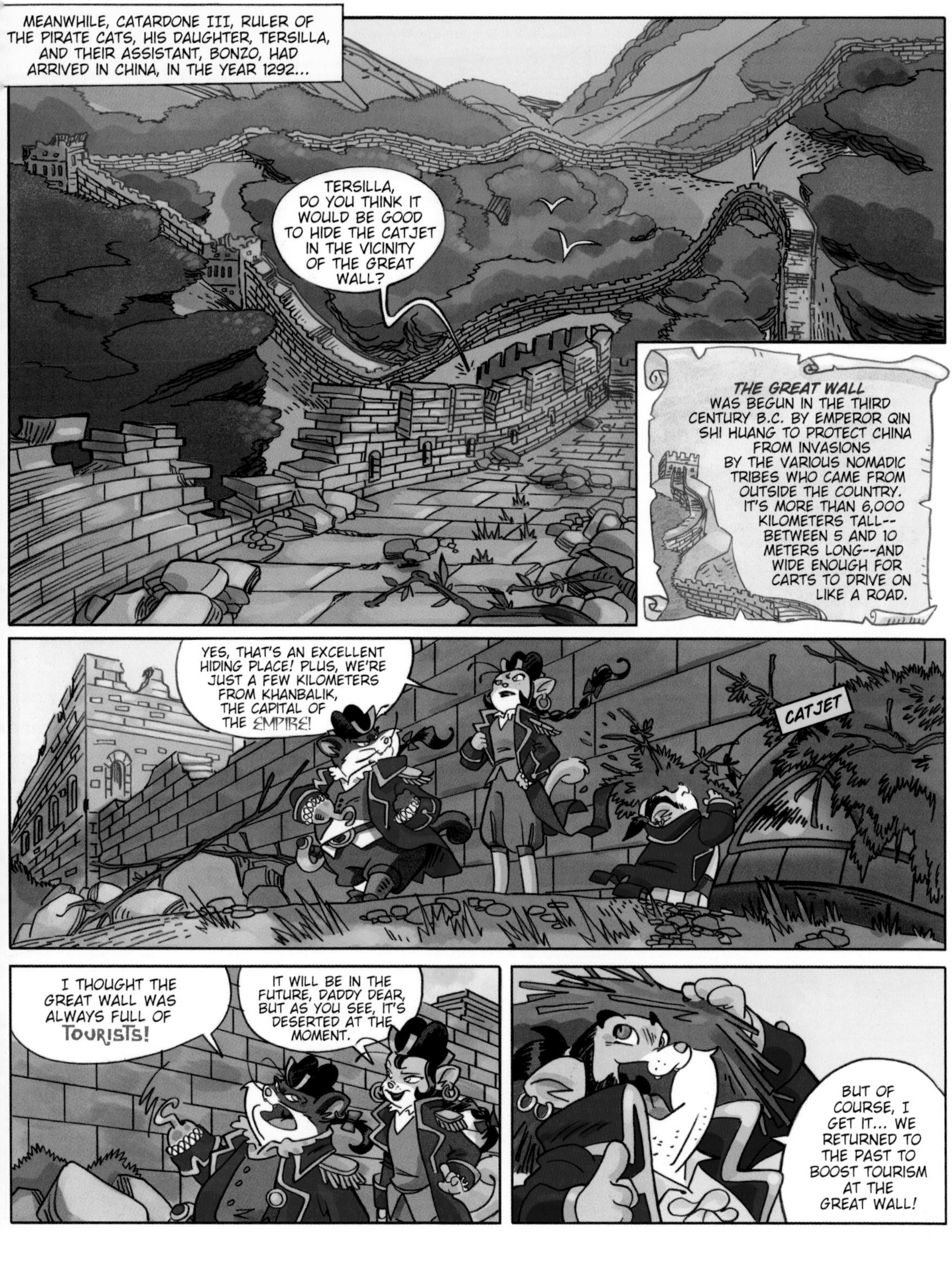
MEANWHILE, CATARDONE III, RULER OF THE PIRATE CATS, HIS DAUGHTER, TERSILLA, AND THEIR ASSISTANT, BONZO, HAD ARRIVED IN CHINA, IN THE YEAR 1292...
TERSILLA, DO YOU THINK IT WOULD BE GOOD TO HIDE THE CATJET IN THE VICINITY OF THE GREAT WALL?
THE GREAT WALL WAS BEGUN IN THE THIRD CENTURY B.C. BY EMPEROR QIN SHI HUANG TO PROTECT CHINA FROM INVASIONS BY THE VARIOUS NOMADIC TRIBES WHO CAME FROM OUTSIDE THE COUNTRY. IT'S MORE THAN 6,000 KILOMETERS TALL--BETWEEN 5 AND 10 METERS LONG--AND WIDE ENOUGH FOR CARTS TO DRIVE ON LIKE A ROAD.
YES, THAT'S AN EXCELLENT HIDING PLACE! PLUS, WE'RE JUST A FEW KILOMETERS FROM KHANBALIK, THE CAPITAL OF THE EMPIRE!
CATJET
I THOUGHT THE GREAT WALL WAS ALWAYS FULL OF TOURISTS!
IT WILL BE IN THE FUTURE, DADDY DEAR, BUT AS YOU SEE, IT'S DESERTED AT THE MOMENT.
BUT OF COURSE, I GET IT... WE RETURNED TO THE PAST TO BOOST TOURISM AT THE GREAT WALL!

GOOD IDEA! TO START WITH, LET'S BUILD A FIVE-STAR HOTEL!

SURE! THE HOTEL "CATARDONE!"

AND A SUPER-DELUXE RESTAURANT NEARBY!

AND A FAIR-GROUND!

QUIIIIIET, YOU TWO!!!

WE'RE DOING NOTHING OF THE KIND! THE MISSION OBJECTIVE IS SOMETHING ELSE!

AH, REALLY?

TOO BAD!

HOW MANY TIMES DO I HAVE TO TELL YOU: WE HAVE TO STEAL THE *diary* OF MARCO POLO, THE GREAT VENETIAN VOYAGER!

WHAT ARE WE GOING TO DO WITH A DIARY?

IT'S JUST A *pile* OF PAPER!

WE'LL PUBLISH IT OURSELVES, SO WE CAN TAKE CREDIT FOR HIS TRAVELS! THAT WAY, THE PIRATE CATS' NAME WILL BE FAMOUS THROUGHOUT THE CENTURIES!

HMM... OF COURSE...

ON THE HOTEL ROOF THERE SHOULD BE A HELICOPTER PAD!

SURE! AND ALSO ONE FOR HOT AIR BALLOONS!

GRRR!

I TOLD YOU TO BE QUIET!!!

16

WE'LL DO WHAT I SAID! STOP MOUSING OFF!*

* TALKING NONSENSE

PHEW... OKAY! BUT HOW ARE WE GOING TO GET NEAR THIS MARCO POLO?

I THOUGHT YOU'D STUDIED UP BEFORE LEAVING, DADDY DEAR!

STU...? WHAT DO YOU MEAN, TERSILLA?

STUDIED, MY EMPEROR, MEANS...

I KNOW PERFECTLY WELL WHAT IT MEANS, *YOU HAIRBALL!* I DON'T NEED A LESSON!

SMACK

AT THIS TIME, CHINA WAS PART OF THE MONGOLIAN EMPIRE! EMPEROR KUBLAI KHAN HOSTED MARCO POLO, HIS FATHER, AND HIS UNCLE!

MONGOLIANS

MONGOLIANS WERE A NOMADIC WARRIOR PEOPLE WHO LIVED IN VARIOUS REGIONS OF CENTRAL ASIA. IN THE EARLY 1200S, THE FAMOUS LEADER GENGHIS KHAN (AROUND 1167-1227) SUCCEEDED IN UNIFYING THE DIFFERENT TRIBES AND BEGAN A WAR OF CONQUEST THAT LED THEM TO OCCUPY THE MAJORITY OF THE CONTINENT OF ASIA, CREATING THE GREATEST EMPIRE HISTORY HAS EVER RECORDED. AFTER GENGHIS KHAN'S DEATH, THE EMPIRE CONTINUED TO EXIST, LASTING UNTIL 1336. TODAY THE DESCENDANTS OF THE MONGOLIAN PEOPLE LIVE IN MONGOLIA, A NATION ON THE BORDER OF CHINA.

TO GET NEAR HIM, WE'LL PRESENT OURSELVES TO COURT, PRETENDING TO BE VENETIAN MERCHANTS! THEN IT'LL BE CHILD'S PLAY TO STEAL THE DIARY!

IS EVERYTHING CLEAR NOW OR DO I HAVE TO EXPLAIN IT TO YOU AGAIN?

YES, YES... THAT IS... NO, THAT IS...

STOP CHATTERING! LET'S PUT ON OUR MOUSE MASKS AND CHANGE CLOTHES!

THIS TIME, NO ONE WILL BE ABLE TO *DERAIL US!*

A LITTLE LATER, ON THE WAY TO KHANBALIK...

I'M TIRED! IS IT MUCH FARTHER?

COME ON! WALK!

IF WE HAD HORSES, IT WOULD BE A LOT EASIER!

LOOK! WE COULD TAKE THOSE DONKEYS OVER THERE!

THOSE AREN'T DONKEYS! THEY'RE PRZEWALSKI'S HORSES!

PRZEWALSKI'S HORSES

ARE A TYPE OF HORSE NATIVE TO MONGOLIA. THEY HAVE A MASSIVE HEAD, WITH SMALL EYES AND EARS, A SQUAT BODY AND A SHORT BRISTLY MANE. THEIR LEGS AND MUZZLES ARE DARKER THAN THE REST OF THEIR BODIES. THE PHYSICAL FEATURES OF THIS HORSE HAVE STAYED THE SAME FROM PREHISTORY TO OUR TIME.

THERE ARE EXACTLY THREE... LIKE US! WHAT DO YOU SAY?

AND HOW ARE WE GOING TO...?

I'LL *RUSH* OVER RIGHT NOW TO CAPTURE THEM! IT'LL JUST TAKE ME A MINUTE!

BONZO, WAIT!

CHARRRGE!!!

THE GIANT PANDA BELONGS TO THE BEAR FAMILY AND EATS ALMOST EXCLUSIVELY BAMBOO. NATIVE TO CENTRAL CHINA, IT CAN ALSO BE FOUND IN THE MOUNTAINOUS REGIONS OF SZECHUAN AND TIBET. TODAY THE PANDA IS AN ENDANGERED SPECIES.

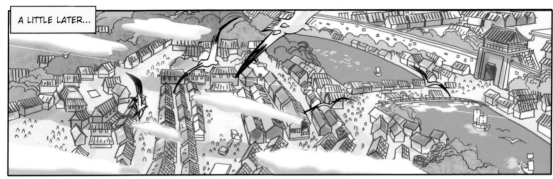

A LITTLE LATER...

→HMFF, HMFF←... IF I RUN ANOTHER FOOT, I'LL **BURST!**

OF COURSE...BUT LUCKILY THE PANDA STOPPED FOLLOWING US AT THE GATES OF KHANBALIK!

→PANT... PANT...←

HUH? YOU SAID KHANBALIK? SO YOU'RE SAYING THAT WE'VE ARRIVED, TERSILLA?

RIGHT, DADDY DEAR!

KHANBALIK (THE CITY OF KHAN)

WAS THE MONGOLIAN NAME USED FOR THE CITY THAT TODAY WE CALL BEIJING. THE FIRST CITY CENTER DATES BACK TO THE 5TH CENTURY B.C. AND WAS FORMED FROM A GROUP OF SMALL VILLAGES. OVER TIME, THE CITY GREW IN IMPORTANCE UNTIL THE MONGOLS CHOSE IT AS THE CAPITAL OF THEIR EMPIRE IN 1267.

HAVE YOU NOTICED EVERYONE'S **LOOKING** AT US?

REMEMBER WE LOOK LIKE VENETIAN MERCHANTS! NOW LET'S GO PRESENT OURSELVES AT COURT!

AT THE COURT OF THE GREAT KHAN...

LET THE FOREIGNERS ENTER!

20

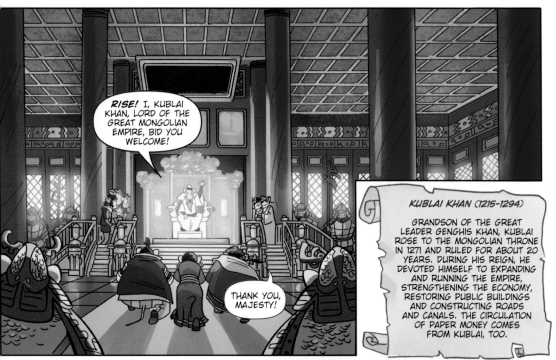

RISE! I, KUBLAI KHAN, LORD OF THE GREAT MONGOLIAN EMPIRE, BID YOU WELCOME!

THANK YOU, MAJESTY!

KUBLAI KHAN (1215-1294)

GRANDSON OF THE GREAT LEADER GENGHIS KHAN, KUBLAI ROSE TO THE MONGOLIAN THRONE IN 1271 AND RULED FOR ABOUT 20 YEARS. DURING HIS REIGN, HE DEVOTED HIMSELF TO EXPANDING AND RUNNING THE EMPIRE, STRENGTHENING THE ECONOMY, RESTORING PUBLIC BUILDINGS AND CONSTRUCTING ROADS AND CANALS. THE CIRCULATION OF PAPER MONEY COMES FROM KUBLAI, TOO.

I AM ALWAYS HAPPY TO WELCOME FOREIGN TRAVELERS! THEY CAN LEARN MANY THINGS FROM ENCOUNTERING OTHER CULTURES!

AND YOU AND YOUR LOVED ONES KNOW THIS WELL, CORRECT, MARCO?

YES, MY LORD!

MARCO? THEN HE MUST BE **MARCO POLO!**

YOU'RE MARCO POLO, WHO LEFT VENICE 20 YEARS AGO WITH YOUR FATHER, NICCOLO, AND YOUR UNCLE, MATTEO?

THAT'S RIGHT! BUT... HOW DID YOU GET TO KNOW MY NAME?

OH, IN **VENICE**, THE CITY WE COME FROM, THE POLO NAME IS VERY FAMOUS!

B-BUT THEN ARE YOU MY COUNTRY-MEN? IT'S SUCH A PLEASURE TO MEET YOU! WHAT'S YOUR NAME?

MY NAME IS RATILLA RATINI AND THIS IS MY FATHER RATARDONE AND OUR FRIEND RATONZO RATON. WE'RE MERCHANTS!

VERY PLEASED TO MEET YOU! THIS IS MY FATHER, NICCOLO, AND MY UNCLE, MATTEO!

WELCOME!

TELL US, WHAT'S THE NEWS FROM VENICE?

DOES OUR BELOVED CITY STILL HAVE THE MOST POWERFUL FLEET ON ALL THE SEAS?

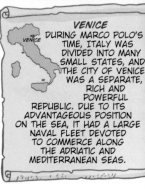

VENICE
DURING MARCO POLO'S TIME, ITALY WAS DIVIDED INTO MANY SMALL STATES, AND THE CITY OF VENICE WAS A SEPARATE, RICH AND POWERFUL REPUBLIC. DUE TO ITS ADVANTAGEOUS POSITION ON THE SEA, IT HAD A LARGE NAVAL FLEET DEVOTED TO COMMERCE ALONG THE ADRIATIC AND MEDITERRANEAN SEAS.

WELL, NOW... IT SEEMS TO ME THAT... AH, YES... THE FLEET *SANK!*

THAT'S RIGHT, BUT... THEY REPLACED IT WITH HELICOPTERS!

WHAT? THE ENTIRE FLEET SANK?

HELICOPTERS? WHAT COULD THESE HELICOPTERS BE?

PLEASE FORGIVE THEM! THEY'RE WORN OUT FROM THE JOURNEY AND DON'T KNOW WHAT THEY'RE SAYING!

-MMPH!-

IN FACT, IF THE GREAT KHAN WILL PERMIT IT, WE'D LIKE TO GO AND REST!

AS YOU WISH! I SHALL ORDER A ROOM BE PREPARED FOR YOU IN THE APARTMENTS RESERVED FOR GUESTS! UNTIL LATER!

AT EXACTLY THE SAME MOMENT, NOT FAR FROM KHANBALIK...

VRROOOOMM

BRAKE, TRAP! WE'RE GOING TO HIT SOMETHING!

I'M TRYING!

WHRRRRR

THE RICE PADDIES! THE RICE PADDIES!

BABOOOMMM

SKREEECH

DID YOU SEE THAT PERFECT LANDING? YOU DIDN'T NEED TO GET ALL WORKED UP!

‑SIGH‑

NEXT TIME, LET PETUNIA DRIVE, PLEASE!

WHAT ARE YOU COMPLAINING ABOUT, COUSIN? LOOK, THE FRIDGE IS SAFE AND SOUND!

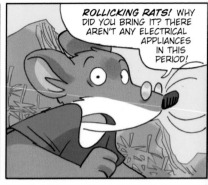

ROLLICKING RATS! WHY DID YOU BRING IT? THERE AREN'T ANY ELECTRICAL APPLIANCES IN THIS PERIOD!

I KNOW, BUT WHO KNOWS? MAYBE IT'LL TURN OUT TO BE USEFUL TO US, AND NO ONE WILL NOTICE IT INSIDE THIS BAG!

IT WOULD BE GOOD TO GET GOING NOW! THE PIRATE CATS ALREADY HAVE ENOUGH OF AN ADVANTAGE!

YOU'RE RIGHT, PATTY, WE'D BETTER NOT LOSE ANY MORE TIME! LET'S GO!

AFTER A QUICK CHANGE OF CLOTHES...

⇒SIGH⇐... THIS TIME PROFESSOR VON VOLT DIDN'T GUESS THE RIGHT SIZE!

TEE, HEE, HEE!

I'LL ROLL UP YOUR SLEEVES LIKE THIS SO YOU'LL BE MORE COMFORTABLE!

UM... THANKS, PETUNIA!

UNCLE GERONIMO, WHERE CAN WE HIDE THE TIME MACHINE?

WHAT DO YOU THINK OF PUTTING IT IN THIS BAMBOO GROVE? IT SHOULDN'T ATTRACT ATTENTION THERE!

THAT SEEMS PERFECT TO ME!

24

AFTER HIDING THE SPEEDRAT, WE FINALLY SET OUT...

THESE RICE PADDIES ARE SO PEACEFUL...

HELPPPPP! WHO CAN HELP ME???

???

MAYBE YOU SPOKE TOO SOON!

GET OFF YOUR HORSE, RIGHT NOW!

HEY LOOK! THAT RODENT IS IN **DANGER!**

GIVE US ALL YOUR MONEY, RODENT!

HOW DARE YOU, SCOUNDRELS? I'M AN IMPERIAL OFFICIAL: THE GREAT KHAN WILL PUNISH YOU FOR THIS!

GET YOUR PAWS OFF HIM!

?

FOR ALL THE EMPEROR'S RICE! FOREIGNERS!

TAKE THAT!

WOOSH

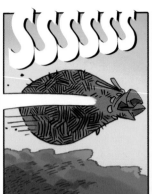

SSSSSSS

BONK!

SQUEEEAK!

OOPS! I AIMED WRONG...

LET'S GET OUT OF HERE! THESE FOREIGNERS ARE A BIT STRANGE!

I'M SO SORRY, COUSIN... I WANTED TO HIT THE THIEVES NOT YOU!

~GROAN!~

WAS THAT WHAT YOU HAD IN MIND WHEN YOU SAID THE FRIDGE MIGHT BE USEFUL TO US?

NO, I ASSURE YOU!

ARE YOU HURT?

NO, AND IT'S ALL THANKS TO YOU! WHO ARE YOU? WHERE ARE YOU FROM?

ALLOW ME TO MAKE THE INTRODUCTIONS! MY NAME IS STILTONIN, GERONIMO STILTONIN...

...AND THESE ARE MY FRIENDS: MISTRESS * PETUNIANA, BUGSORAMA, BENJAMINO, AND TRAPOLON! WE'RE MERCHANTS AND WE COME FROM VENICE!

*MISTRESS/ MISS, IN OLD ITALIAN.

26

VENICE, DID YOU SAY? THEN YOU COME FROM THE SAME CITY AS THE POLOS!

UM...THAT'S RIGHT! AND WHO ARE YOU, IF I MIGHT ASK?

MY NAME IS MOUSE-CHECHUNG AND I'M AN OFFICIAL FOR THE *GREAT KHAN!*

OFFICIALS

IN ORDER TO ADMINISTER HIS VERY VAST KINGDOM, THE GREAT KHAN USED MANY OFFICIALS. THEY TRAVELED CONSTANTLY THROUGHOUT THE ENTIRE EMPIRE, WORKING TO CONVEY HIS COMMANDS TO THE GOVERNORS OF THE DIFFERENT PROVINCES.

TELL US, MOUSE-CHECHUNG, DO YOU KNOW MARCO POLO? HIS FATHER AND UNCLE SHOULD BE WITH HIM, TOO.

ABSOLUTELY! I'VE CARRIED OUT MORE THAN ONE DIPLOMATIC MISSION FOR THE GREAT KHAN WITH YOUNG MARCO!

WE'D LOVE TO MEET HIM! EVERYONE IN VENICE HAS BEEN ASKING WHAT BECAME OF THE POLOS!

IF YOU COME WITH ME TO KHANBALIK, I'D BE HAPPY TO INTRODUCE THEM TO YOU!

YOU'RE VERY KIND!

I'LL INTRODUCE YOU TO THE GREAT KHAN, TOO! HE'S ALWAYS GLAD TO WELCOME TRAVELERS WHO COME FROM DIFFERENT LANDS!

IT WOULD BE A GREAT honor FOR US IF WE WERE ABLE TO ENTER THE COURT OF THE GREAT KHAN!

FOLLOW ME! IF WE WALK AT A GOOD PACE, WE'LL BE IN KHANBALIK THIS AFTERNOON!

SO WE ARRIVED AT THE IMPERIAL PALACE IN THE MAGNIFICENT ROYAL CITY OF KHANBALIK...

THE IMPERIAL PALACE

ROSE FROM INSIDE A DOUBLY WALLED-IN AREA. BASED ON MARCO POLO'S DESCRIPTION, IT WAS IMMENSE, AND THE WALLS OF ITS ROOMS WERE COVERED WITH SILVER AND GOLD. THERE WERE GARDENS AND A LAKE, FED BY A RIVER. IN ADDITION, JUST BEHIND THE PALACE, THE KHAN HAD BUILT AN ARTIFICIAL HILL, ON WHICH TREES FROM EVERY REGION IN THE EMPIRE WERE PLANTED.

...HOME OF KUBLAI KHAN, LORD OF THE VASTEST EMPIRE HISTORY HAS EVER RECORDED!

MORE VENETIAN MERCHANTS HAVE ARRIVED?

THIS IS REALLY A DAY OF SURPRISES!

?!?

IT'S A PITY... ANOTHER THREE VENETIAN MERCHANTS ARRIVED AT COURT TODAY, BUT THEY'VE JUST LEFT FOR THE CITY OF QUINSAI, ALONG WITH MARCO POLO!

QUINSAI

WAS THE ANCIENT NAME OF THE MODERN-DAY CITY OF HANGZHOU. BUILT ON THE YANGTZE RIVER DELTA (THE BLUE RIVER), ITS LANDSCAPE LOOKS A LOT LIKE VENICE, WITH MANY BRIDGES AND CANALS. MARCO POLO WAS VERY FOND OF THE SPOT AND SPOKE OF IT AS ONE OF THE MOST BEAUTIFUL AND NOBLE CITIES IN THE WORLD.

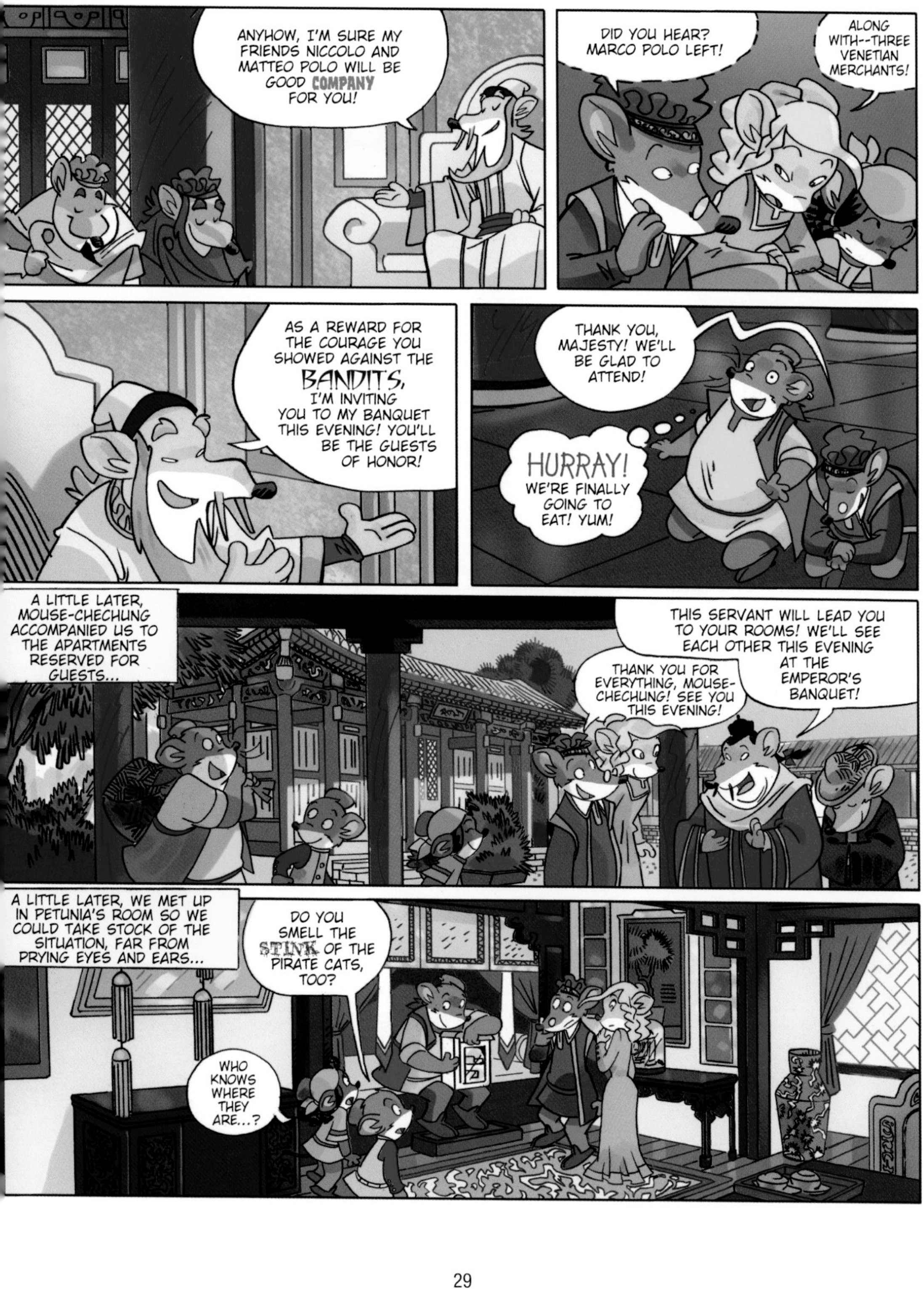

ANYHOW, I'M SURE MY FRIENDS NICCOLO AND MATTEO POLO WILL BE GOOD COMPANY FOR YOU!
DID YOU HEAR? MARCO POLO LEFT!
ALONG WITH--THREE VENETIAN MERCHANTS!
AS A REWARD FOR THE COURAGE YOU SHOWED AGAINST THE BANDITS, I'M INVITING YOU TO MY BANQUET THIS EVENING! YOU'LL BE THE GUESTS OF HONOR!
THANK YOU, MAJESTY! WE'LL BE GLAD TO ATTEND!
HURRAY! WE'RE FINALLY GOING TO EAT! YUM!
A LITTLE LATER, MOUSE-CHECHUNG ACCOMPANIED US TO THE APARTMENTS RESERVED FOR GUESTS...
THIS SERVANT WILL LEAD YOU TO YOUR ROOMS! WE'LL SEE EACH OTHER THIS EVENING AT THE EMPEROR'S BANQUET!
THANK YOU FOR EVERYTHING, MOUSE-CHECHUNG! SEE YOU THIS EVENING!
A LITTLE LATER, WE MET UP IN PETUNIA'S ROOM SO WE COULD TAKE STOCK OF THE SITUATION, FAR FROM PRYING EYES AND EARS...
DO YOU SMELL THE STINK OF THE PIRATE CATS, TOO?
WHO KNOWS WHERE THEY ARE...?

WHEN KUBLAI KHAN MENTIONED THREE MERCHANTS, A **SHIVER** RAN ALONG MY FUR!

PHEW! YOU'RE A REGULAR 'FRAIDY-MOUSE, COUSIN!

BUT THEIR ARRIVAL IS A REALLY STRANGE COINCIDENCE! WE SHOULD **INVESTIGATE!**

I AGREE WITH YOU, *PETUNIA!*

IMAGINE IF YOU DIDN'T!

>PHEW...< WHERE WERE THE THREE MERCHANTS HEADED?

TO *CHUNCHAI,* I THINK...

NO, IT WAS QUINSAI!

AND MARCO POLO WAS WITH THEM!

THAT'S STRANGE, TOO! THEY'VE JUST BARELY ARRIVED FROM A LONG JOURNEY AND HAVE ALREADY LEFT AGAIN! IT ALMOST SEEMS AS IF...

...THEY DIDN'T WANT TO LOSE SIGHT OF MARCO POLO!

IT REALLY SEEMS LIKE... BUT IF THIS IS REALLY ABOUT THE PIRATE CATS, WHAT CAN THEY WANT WITH HIM?

THE ONLY WAY TO KNOW IS FOR US TO GO TO QUINSAI TOO, AND KEEP OUR EYES WIDE OPEN! THEY COULD BE ANYWHERE!

THAT'S FINE WITH ME, BUT NOT BEFORE THE GREAT KHAN'S BANQUET: THE FRIDGE IS ALMOST **EMPTY!**

TSK!

THAT EVENING, DURING THE MAGNIFICENT BANQUET GIVEN BY THE EMPEROR...

...I TOOK ADVANTAGE OF THE OPPORTUNITY TO CONSULT WITH MOUSE-CHECHUNG AND THE POLO BROTHERS.

SO YOU WANT TO GO TO THE CITY OF QUINSAI, TOO?

WE'D LIKE TO VISIT IT AND MEET YOUR *SON!*

WOW! YOU'RE REALLY TIRELESS TRAVELERS!

THE ROUTE IS RATHER LONG: IT WILL TAKE AROUND A MONTH ON HORSEBACK! WHEN DO YOU WANT TO LEAVE?

TOMORROW **MORNING** IF POSSIBLE!

IT SHOULD BE. I'LL TALK TO THE KHAN ABOUT IT. I THINK HE'LL AGREE I SHOULD GO WITH YOU MYSELF!

THANKS, MOUSE-CHECHUNG, YOU'RE A REAL GENTLE-MOUSE!

THE FOLLOWING DAY, HAVING GOTTEN THE KHAN'S PERMISSION, WE STARTED OFF...

HOW COME MARCO POLO LEFT THE COURT OF THE KHAN TO GO TO QUINSAI?

MARCO **ADORES** THAT CITY! HE GOES TO VISIT IT VERY OFTEN!

AND NOW, SINCE HE'LL BE RETURNING TO EUROPE SOON, HE ASKED THE GREAT KHAN TO LET HIM SEE IT ONE LAST TIME!

SO MARCO AND HIS **FAMILY** HAVE ALREADY ARRANGED TO GO BACK TO VENICE?

YES, THE POLOS HAVE WANTED TO FOR SOME TIME NOW! BUT THE KHAN IS VERY ATTACHED TO THEM AND DIDN'T WANT TO PART FROM THEM!

IT WAS ONLY A FEW DAYS AGO THAT HE GAVE HIS AGREEMENT TO LET THEM LEAVE FOR VENICE!

I UNDERSTAND THE POLOS. I, TOO, WOULDN'T WANT TO STAY FAR AWAY FOREVER FROM NEW MOUSE... AHEM... FROM VENICE!

OF COURSE... AS ONE OF OUR PROVERBS SAYS, "THERE'S A TIME TO FISH AND A TIME TO BRING IN THE NETS!" AND NOW IS THE TIME FOR THEM TO RETURN!

THE FOLLOWING DAY, WE RODE FROM DAWN TO DUSK, STOPPING ONLY TO REST AND CHANGE HORSES...

THE NETWORK OF ROADS
THE MONGOLIAN EMPIRE HAD A SYSTEM OF ROADS THAT WAS VERY ADVANCED FOR THE TIME. STREETS RAN FROM KHANBALIK TO THE ENTIRE EMPIRE, PASSABLE ON FOOT OR HORSEBACK. ALONG THE ROADS WERE STATIONS WHERE THE KHAN'S MESSENGERS COULD REST AND CHANGE HORSES BEFORE CONTINUING ON TOWARDS THEIR DESTINATIONS.

THE JOURNEY WAS PEACEFUL, EXCEPT FOR A FEW TINY INCIDENTS...

YIIIKES!

AAHHHHHH!

CLOMP

CLOMP

CLOMP

AAHHH! HELP!

MEANWHILE, WITH A DAY'S HEAD START BEFORE WE LEFT, THE PIRATE CATS HAD REACHED QUINSAI...

...AND HAD SETTLED IN WITH MARCO AT ONE OF THE KHAN'S PALACES.

WHAT **SPLENDOR!** WHAT LUXURY!

INDEED! THE EMPEROR DOESN'T HOLD BACK FROM SPENDING FOR HIS RESIDENCE! AND YOU HAVEN'T SEEN THE GARDENS YET!

BUT YOU MUST'VE SEEN SO MANY INCREDIBLE THINGS DURING YOUR TRAVELS. RIGHT, MARCO?

YES, IT'S TRUE! I'VE TRAVELED THROUGHOUT THE WHOLE EMPIRE AND HAVE SEEN SOME WONDERFUL THINGS!

WE'RE REALLY **CURIOUS** TO HEAR YOUR TALES. RIGHT, RATONZO?

WELL... BY AND LARGE...

MY TALES? ACTUALLY, THEY MIGHT BE VERY INTERESTING FOR WESTERNERS!

OUCH!

BAM!

WHAT DID YOU DO TO REMEMBER EVERYTHING? DID YOU KEEP A DIARY PERHAPS?

OF COURSE, I WROTE DOWN EVERYTHING I SAW AND EVERY EXCITING THING I EXPERIENCED!

FANTASTIC PLACES, NAMES NEVER HEARD BEFORE, INFORMATION ON THE LIVES OF OTHER PEOPLE... BASICALLY THE **LAST 20 YEARS OF MY LIFE!**

AND DO YOU HAVE YOUR DIARY HERE WITH YOU? I WOULD VERY MUCH IN FACT, *VERY, VERY MUCH* LIKE TO READ IT!

WELL... YES... I NEVER PART WITH IT!

MAYBE I'LL READ TO YOU FROM IT LATER! BUT NOW, I BET YOU CAN'T WAIT TO VISIT THE CITY!

OF COURSE! WE CAME WITH YOU FOR JUST THAT REASON!

I'D HAVE PREFERRED FORTY WINKS!

YOU DON'T SAY!

THAT EVENING, AFTER A LONG STROLL THROUGH QUINSAI...

PLEASE, GO IN AND GET YOURSELVES SETTLED.

WHILE YOU'RE HERE, I'LL GET MY DIARY SO YOU CAN LEAF THROUGH IT!

HERE IT IS!

HMMM... IT'S VERY *HEAVY!*

SLAM

35

TIE HIM UP AND GAG HIM!

BONZO, TIE HIM UP AND GAG HIM!

WE'VE DONE IT! MARCO POLO'S DIARY IS OURS!

SEND BONZO TO SADDLE THE HORSES SO WE CAN RETURN TO KHANBALIK AND GET BACK TO THE **CATJET!**

WE'LL LEAVE AT THE FIRST LIGHT OF DAWN... THAT WAY THE GUARDS WON'T SUSPECT US!

AND WHAT SHOULD WE DO WITH MARCO POLO? AREN'T YOU AFRAID SOMEONE WILL FIND HIM AND CHASE AFTER US?

WE'LL TELL THE GUARDS MARCO ORDERED THAT HE NOT BE DISTURBED FOR ANY REASON...

...AND TO BE SAFE, WE'LL GO BACK TO KHANBALIK BY SKIRTING THE IMPERIAL CANAL: IT'S VERY CROWDED THERE AND NO ONE WILL **NOTICE US!**

MMMM! HEL...! MMMPH!

IT LOOKS LIKE OUR FRIEND HAS ALREADY REGAINED CONSCIOUSNESS!

YOU SHOULD HAVE A HARDER HEAD, LIKE BONZO, HEE, HEE, HEE!

HEY!

IT'S BEEN A REAL PLEASURE GETTING TO KNOW YOU, MARCO POLO... GOODBYE AND THANKS!

SMACK

THE NEXT DAY AT DAWN, MY FRIENDS AND I ARRIVED AT QUINSAI...

HERE IT IS! WE'VE REACHED THE PALACE WHERE MARCO POLO IS STAYING!

BRR... THOSE GUARDS LOOK VERY THREATENING!

GOOD MORNING, MY NAME IS MOUSE-CHECHUNG AND I AM AN OFFICIAL TO HIS MAJESTY THE KHAN! MY FRIENDS AND I WOULD LIKE TO SEE MR. MARCO POLO!

I'M SORRY, BUT MARCO POLO ORDERED THAT HE NOT BE DISTURBED!

BUT I'M A CLOSE FRIEND!

AND WE WERE GIVEN AN ORDER! IS THAT CLEEEEAR?

TSK! WHAT RUDE GUARDS!

IS THERE A PROBLEM, MOUSE-CHECHUNG?

UMM... IT SEEMS THAT NO ONE IS ALLOWED TO MEET WITH MARCO POLO FOR THE TIME BEING!

BUT WE *HAVE* TO SEE HIM! IT'S VERY IMPORTANT!

AH...AND HOW COME?

THE TRUTH IS, WE'RE AFRAID THAT MARCO POLO MAY BE IN GRAVE *DANGER!*

IN DANGER?

A BIT UNCOMFORTABLE WITH THE IDEA OF LYING, WE MADE UP A STORY TO JUSTIFY OUR SUSPICIONS...

WHEN WE ARRIVED IN CHINA, WE MET A MERCHANT WHO HAD TRAVELED ALONG THE SILK ROAD: HE TOLD US ABOUT HAVING MET THREE **CATS**...

...WHO BRAGGED TO HIM, SAYING THEY WERE GOING TO BE INTRODUCED AT THE COURT OF THE KHAN, DISGUISED AS MICE!

C-C-CATS???

THE SILK ROAD
WAS A SERIES OF ROUTES THAT CONNECTED CHINA TO THE MIDDLE EAST AND THE MEDITERRANEAN SEA, ALLOWING MERCHANT CARAVANS TO CROSS CENTRAL ASIA. THE MOST COMMONLY TRADED PRODUCTS WERE GOLD, SPICES FOR SEASONING AND PRESERVING FOOD (PEPPER AND NUTMEG) AND VALUABLE CLOTH, INCLUDING SILK WHICH THE ROAD GOT ITS NAME FROM.

RIGHT! WE SUSPECT THEY'RE ACTUALLY THE THREE VENETIAN RODENTS WHO WENT WITH MARCO POLO!

BUT THEN WE HAVE TO WARN MARCO IMMEDIATELY!

IF ONLY THE GUARDS WEREN'T BLOCKING THE DOOR...

THE ONLY SOLUTION IS TO ENTER THE PALACE SECRETLY!

BUT HOW? THE *WALL* IS VERY HIGH!

UMM...

MAYBE YOU COULD TRY TO CLIMB UP AND JUMP OVER THE WALL!

M-ME? YOU KNOW I'M AFRAID OF HEIGHTS!

I'VE GOT A SOLUTION!

?!?

WOW! A CATAPULT!

HUH? A CATAPULT?!?

DO YOU MIND TELLING ME WHERE YOU MANAGED TO FIND IT?

I GOT IT FROM THOSE CRAFTS- MEN OVER THERE!

I TRADED IT FOR THE FRIDGE! THEY DIDN'T UNDER- STAND WHAT IT WAS, BUT THEY'RE USING IT AS AN END TABLE!

YES, BUT WHAT WILL WE DO WITH A CATAPULT? DO YOU WANT TO KNOCK DOWN THE PALACE?

NO, COUSIN! I WAS JUST THINKING OF *FLINGING* YOU OVER THE WALL!

SMAK

HUH?

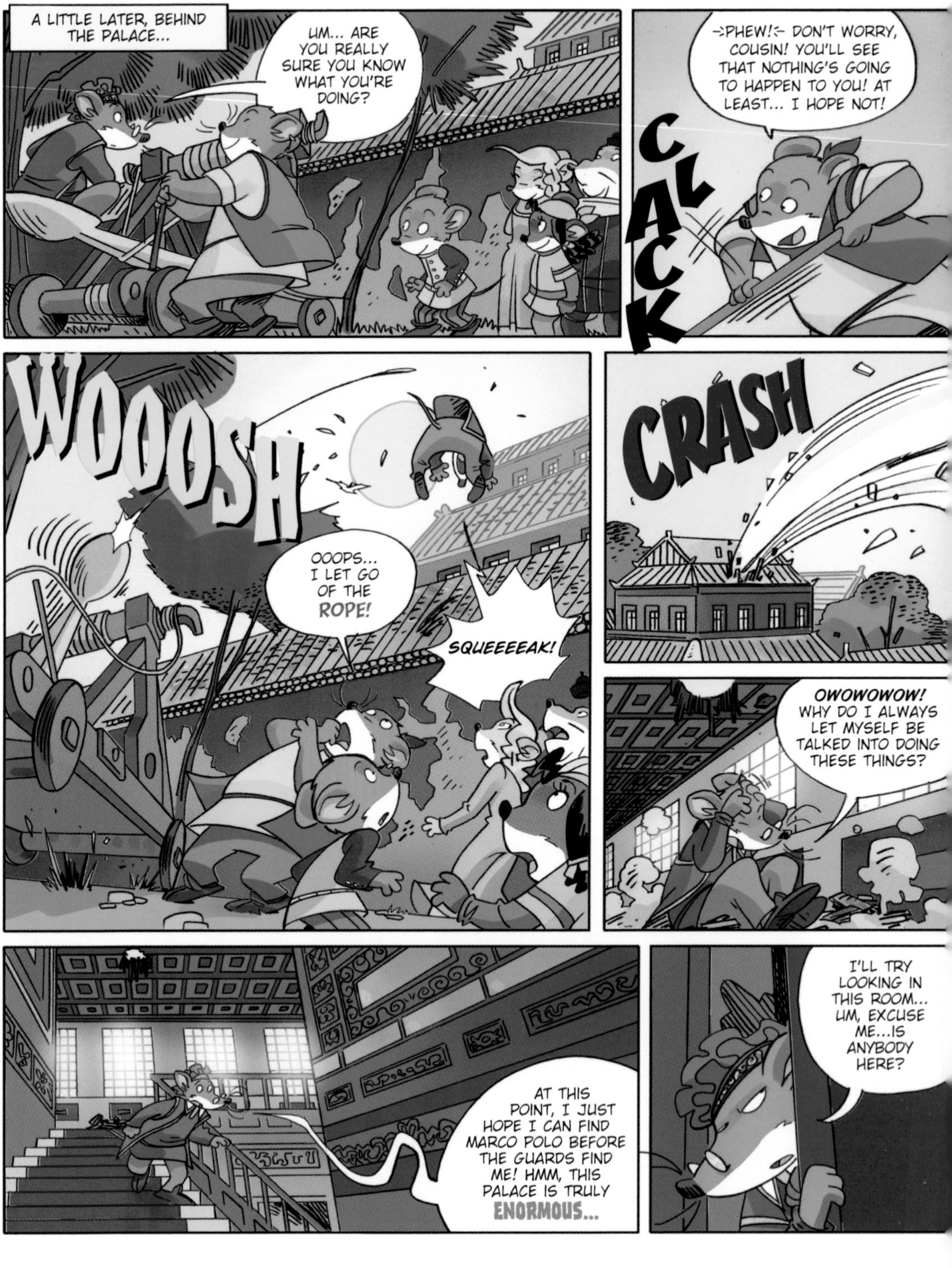
A LITTLE LATER, BEHIND THE PALACE...
UM... ARE YOU REALLY SURE YOU KNOW WHAT YOU'RE DOING?
-PHEW!- DON'T WORRY, COUSIN! YOU'LL SEE THAT NOTHING'S GOING TO HAPPEN TO YOU! AT LEAST... I HOPE NOT!
CLACK
WOOOSH
OOOPS... I LET GO OF THE ROPE!
SQUEEEEAK!
CRASH
OWOWOWOW! WHY DO I ALWAYS LET MYSELF BE TALKED INTO DOING THESE THINGS?
AT THIS POINT, I JUST HOPE I CAN FIND MARCO POLO BEFORE THE GUARDS FIND ME! HMM, THIS PALACE IS TRULY ENORMOUS...
I'LL TRY LOOKING IN THIS ROOM... UM, EXCUSE ME...IS ANYBODY HERE?

MMMMM! MMMMM!

ROTTEN ROQUEFORT!

WAIT, I'LL HAVE YOU FREE IN A MOMENT! WHO WAS IT THAT TIED YOU UP LIKE THIS?

A LITTLE LATER, MARCO ORDERED THAT MY FRIENDS BE LET IN AND TOLD US WHAT HAD HAPPENED...

THERE'S NO LONGER ANY DOUBT ABOUT IT. THEY REALLY ARE THE Pirate Cats! WE'VE GOT TO STOP THEM!

UMM... SINCE IT CONTAINS REPORTS OF MARCO POLO'S TRAVELS, MAYBE THEY WANT TO PUBLISH IT IN HIS PLACE AND TAKE CREDIT FOR IT!

WHO KNOWS WHY THEY STOLE THE DIARY...?

OH, NO! IF THAT'S THE CASE, THEY'LL CHANGE THE COURSE OF HISTORY!

BY CHANCE, DO YOU KNOW WHAT DIRECTION THOSE SCOUNDRELS WERE HEADING?

I HEARD THEY WANTED TO RETURN TO KHANBALIK, SKIRTING THE IMPERIAL CANAL!

WE HAVE TO CATCH UP WITH THEM!

I'M GOING WITH YOU, TOO! I HAVE A SCORE TO SETTLE WITH THOSE THREE SCOUNDRELS!

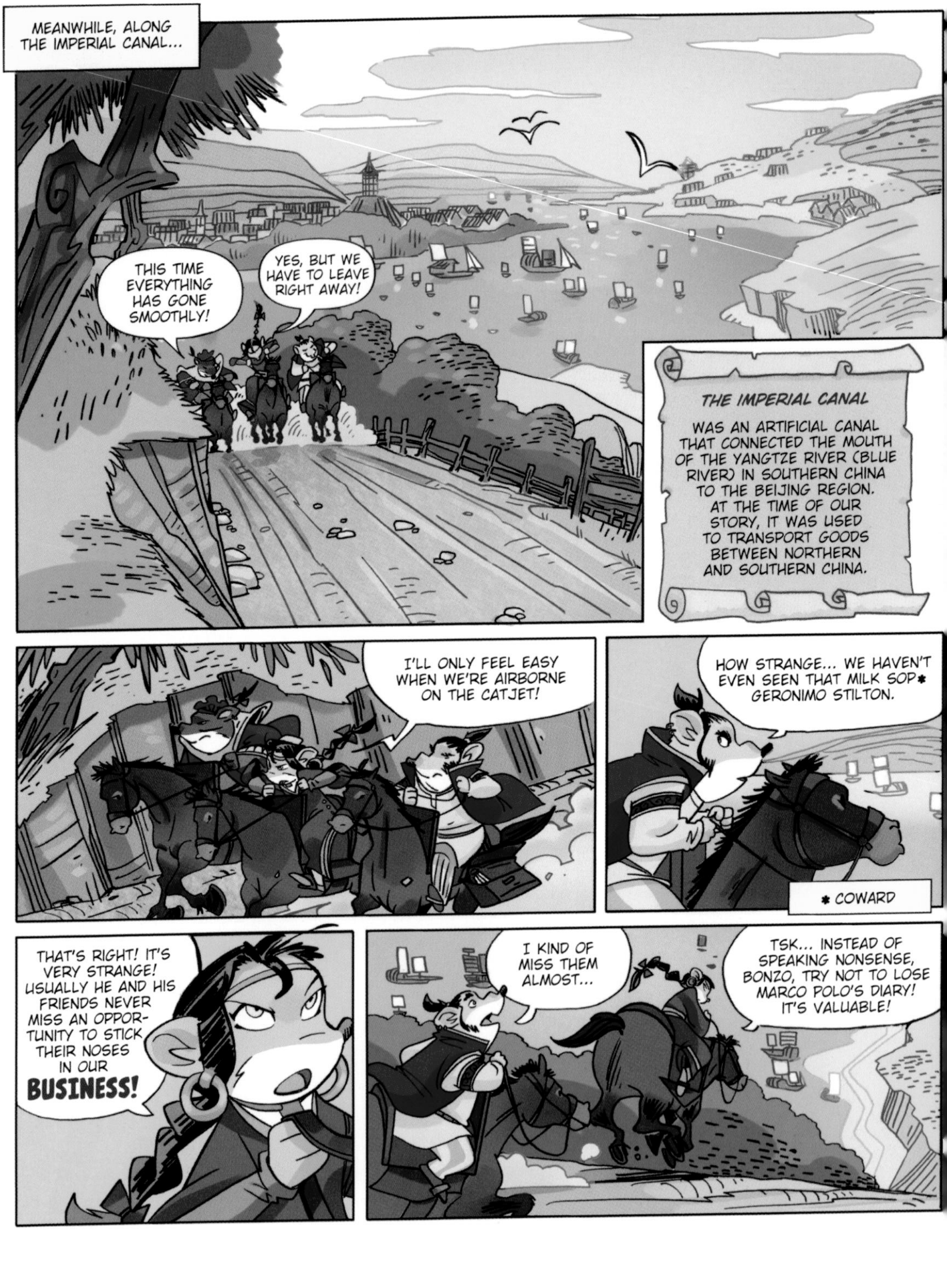
MEANWHILE, ALONG THE IMPERIAL CANAL...
THIS TIME EVERYTHING HAS GONE SMOOTHLY!
YES, BUT WE HAVE TO LEAVE RIGHT AWAY!
THE IMPERIAL CANAL
WAS AN ARTIFICIAL CANAL THAT CONNECTED THE MOUTH OF THE YANGTZE RIVER (BLUE RIVER) IN SOUTHERN CHINA TO THE BEIJING REGION. AT THE TIME OF OUR STORY, IT WAS USED TO TRANSPORT GOODS BETWEEN NORTHERN AND SOUTHERN CHINA.
I'LL ONLY FEEL EASY WHEN WE'RE AIRBORNE ON THE CATJET!
HOW STRANGE... WE HAVEN'T EVEN SEEN THAT MILK SOP* GERONIMO STILTON.
* COWARD
THAT'S RIGHT! IT'S VERY STRANGE! USUALLY HE AND HIS FRIENDS NEVER MISS AN OPPORTUNITY TO STICK THEIR NOSES IN OUR BUSINESS!
I KIND OF MISS THEM ALMOST...
TSK... INSTEAD OF SPEAKING NONSENSE, BONZO, TRY NOT TO LOSE MARCO POLO'S DIARY! IT'S VALUABLE!

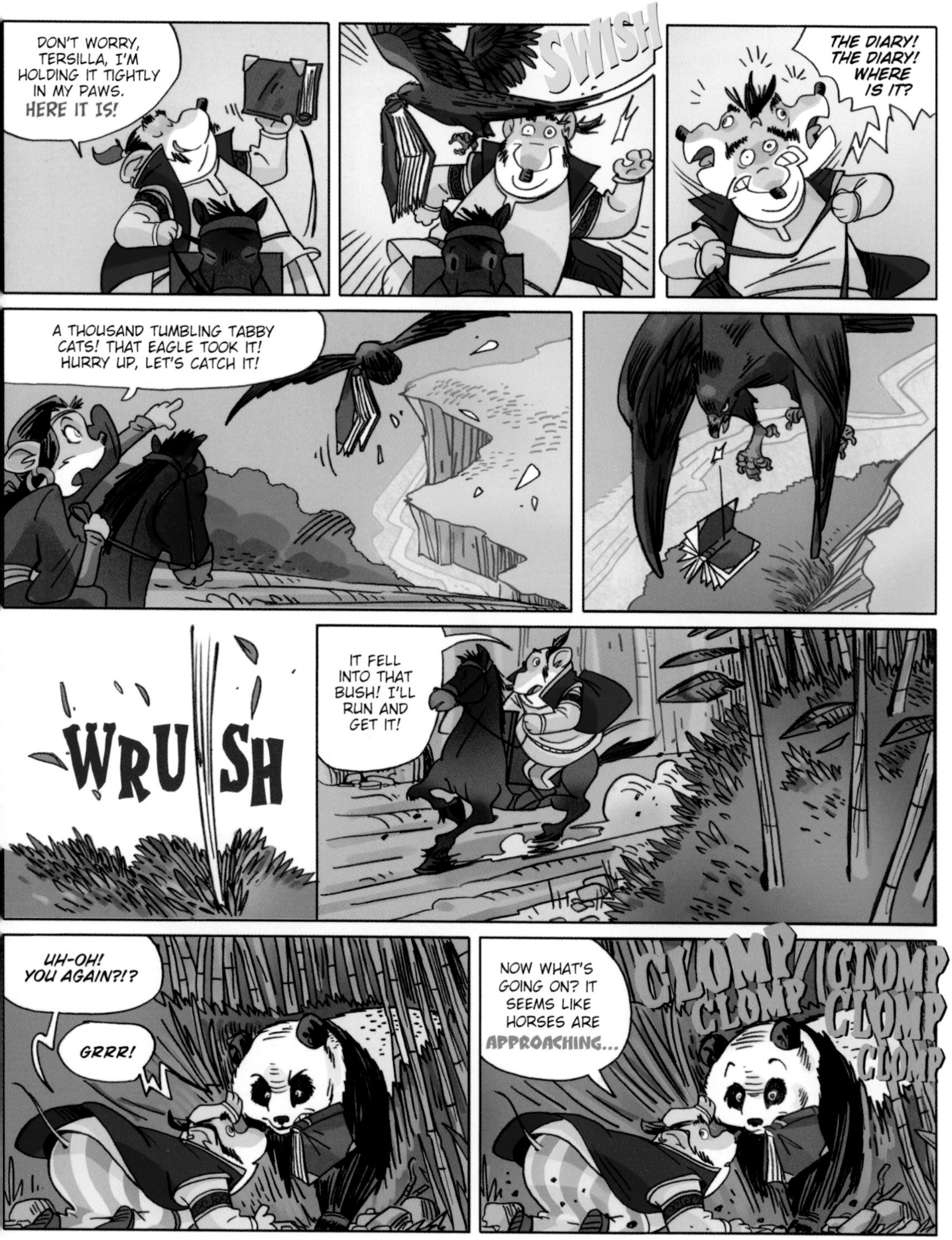

DON'T WORRY, TERSILLA, I'M HOLDING IT TIGHTLY IN MY PAWS. HERE IT IS!
SWISH
THE DIARY! THE DIARY! WHERE IS IT?
A THOUSAND TUMBLING TABBY CATS! THAT EAGLE TOOK IT! HURRY UP, LET'S CATCH IT!
WRUSH
IT FELL INTO THAT BUSH! I'LL RUN AND GET IT!
UH-OH! YOU AGAIN?!?
GRRR!
NOW WHAT'S GOING ON? IT SEEMS LIKE HORSES ARE APPROACHING...
CLOMP CLOMP CLOMP CLOMP CLOMP

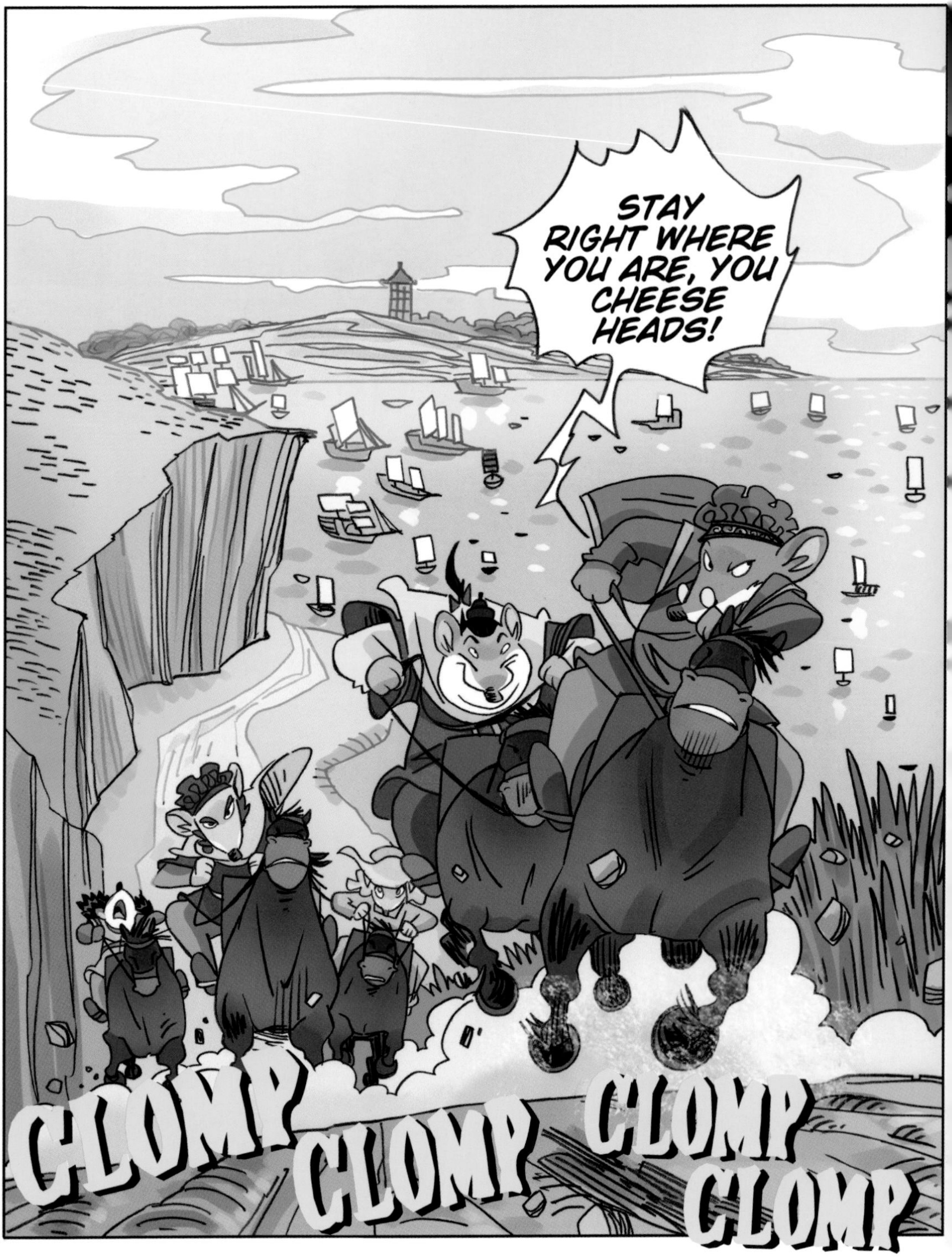
STAY RIGHT WHERE YOU ARE, YOU CHEESE HEADS!
CLOMP CLOMP CLOMP CLOMP

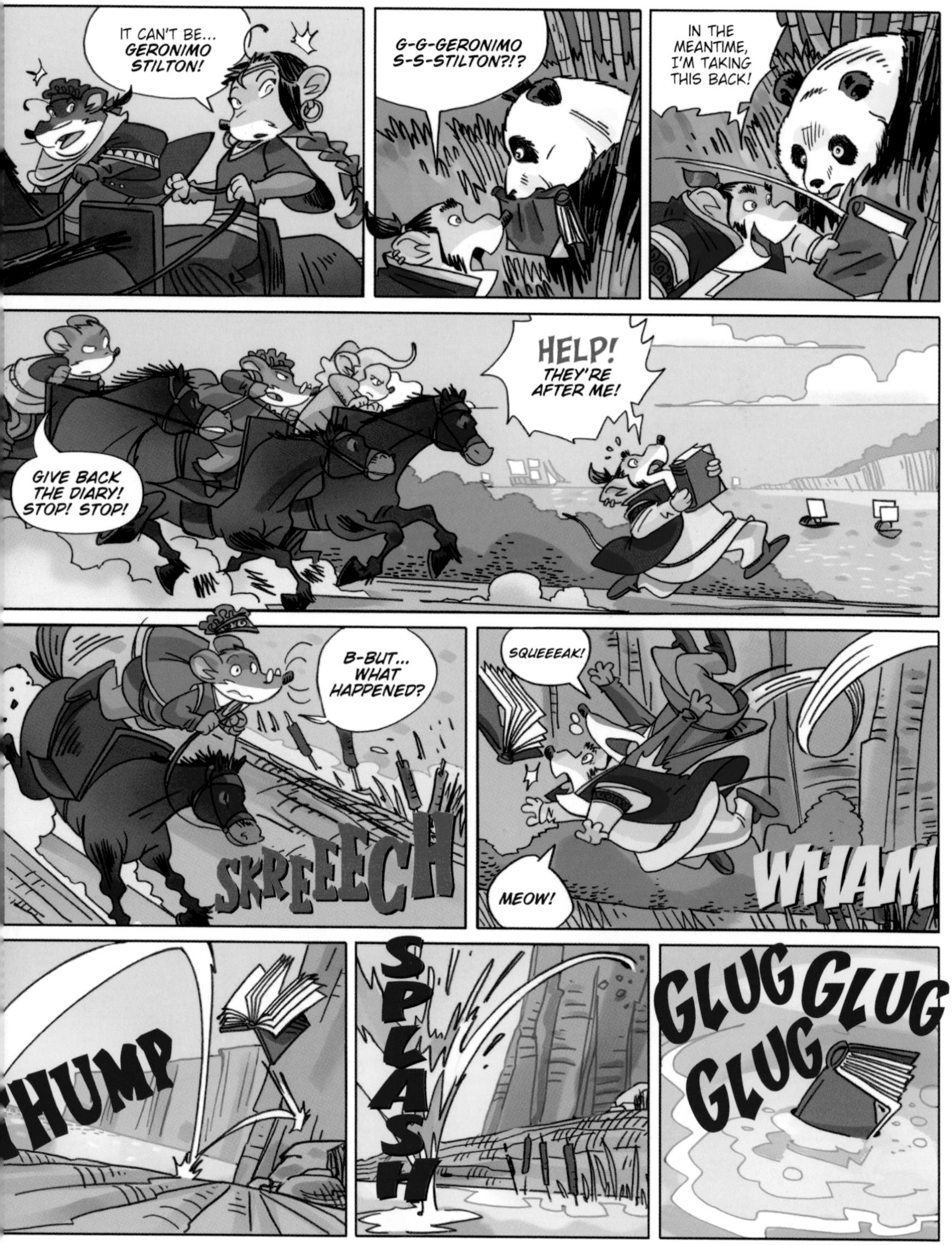
IT CAN'T BE... GERONIMO STILTON!
G-G-GERONIMO S-S-STILTON?!?
IN THE MEANTIME, I'M TAKING THIS BACK!
HELP! THEY'RE AFTER ME!
GIVE BACK THE DIARY! STOP! STOP!
B-BUT... WHAT HAPPENED?
SKREEECH
SQUEEEAK!
MEOW!
WHAM
THUMP
SPLASH
GLUG GLUG GLUG

MY DIARY! IT WOUND UP IN THE *WATER!*

A THOUSAND TUMBLING TABBY CATS! WE ABSOLUTELY HAVE TO GET IT BACK!

I THINK WE'VE GOT A BIG PROBLEM!

BONZO, DON'T JUST STAND THERE LIKE A STICK! WE HAVE TO GET AWAY! *COME ON!*

YES, YES... I'M COMING! WAIT FOR ME!

-*GULP!*-

QUICK! WE CAN'T LET THEM TAKE US! HIYAH!

ENJOY YOUR VICTORY, RATS-IN-MY-BOOTS! BUT YOU WON'T BE ABLE TO STOP US NEXT TIME!

NOW WHAT DO WE DO-- FOLLOW THEM?

IT'S USELESS! THEIR PLAN HAS FIZZLED OUT, LUCKILY!

UM... I'M SO SORRY, MARCO!

CHIN UP, MARCO! AT LEAST WE MANAGED TO GET YOU OUT OF THEIR CLUTCHES!

SO WE'VE COME TO THE END OF OUR ADVENTURE: ONCE AGAIN WE FOILED THE PIRATE CATS' PLAN!

DO I HAVE TO SAY IT TO YOU, BONZO?

YES, TERSILLA, I KNOW... IT'S ALL MY FAULT!

WE WERE ALL UPSET THAT MARCO'S DIARY HAD BEEN LOST AND SPOKE LITTLE DURING OUR RETURN...

I DON'T UNDERSTAND, UNCLE GERONIMO: HOW CAN MARCO POLO *WRITE* HIS TRAVELS WITHOUT THE DIARY?

IT WON'T BE A PROBLEM. HE'LL MANAGE TO DO IT ANYWAY!

ACTUALLY, MARCO POLO DIDN'T HAVE ANY DIARY WITH HIM WHEN HE RETURNED FROM CHINA, BUT THANKS TO HIS **EXCEPTIONAL** MEMORY, HE MANAGED TO REMEMBER AND DICTATE ALL THE ADVENTURES HE'D EXPERIENCED...

...TO AN ITALIAN POET OF THE PERIOD, WHO THEN WROTE *THE TRAVELS OF MARCO POLO!*

WHAT A RELIEF! THEN EVERYTHING'S OKAY!

THE TRAVELS OF MARCO POLO WAS WRITTEN IN 1298, WHILE MARCO WAS A PRISONER OF THE CITY OF GENOA. IT WAS NOT MARCO WHO WROTE THE BOOK, BUT ONE OF HIS FELLOW CELL MATES, RUSTICELLO DA PISA, WHO MARCO TOLD ABOUT HIS ADVENTURES. IN 1299, MARCO WAS SET FREE AND RETURNED TO VENICE; THE BOOK WAS PUBLISHED IN OLD FRENCH. LATER ON, IT WAS CALLED IL MILIONE, PERHAPS DUE TO THE NAME "EMILIONE," IN REMEMBRANCE OF AN ANCESTOR IN THE POLO FAMILY WHO WAS CALLED THAT.

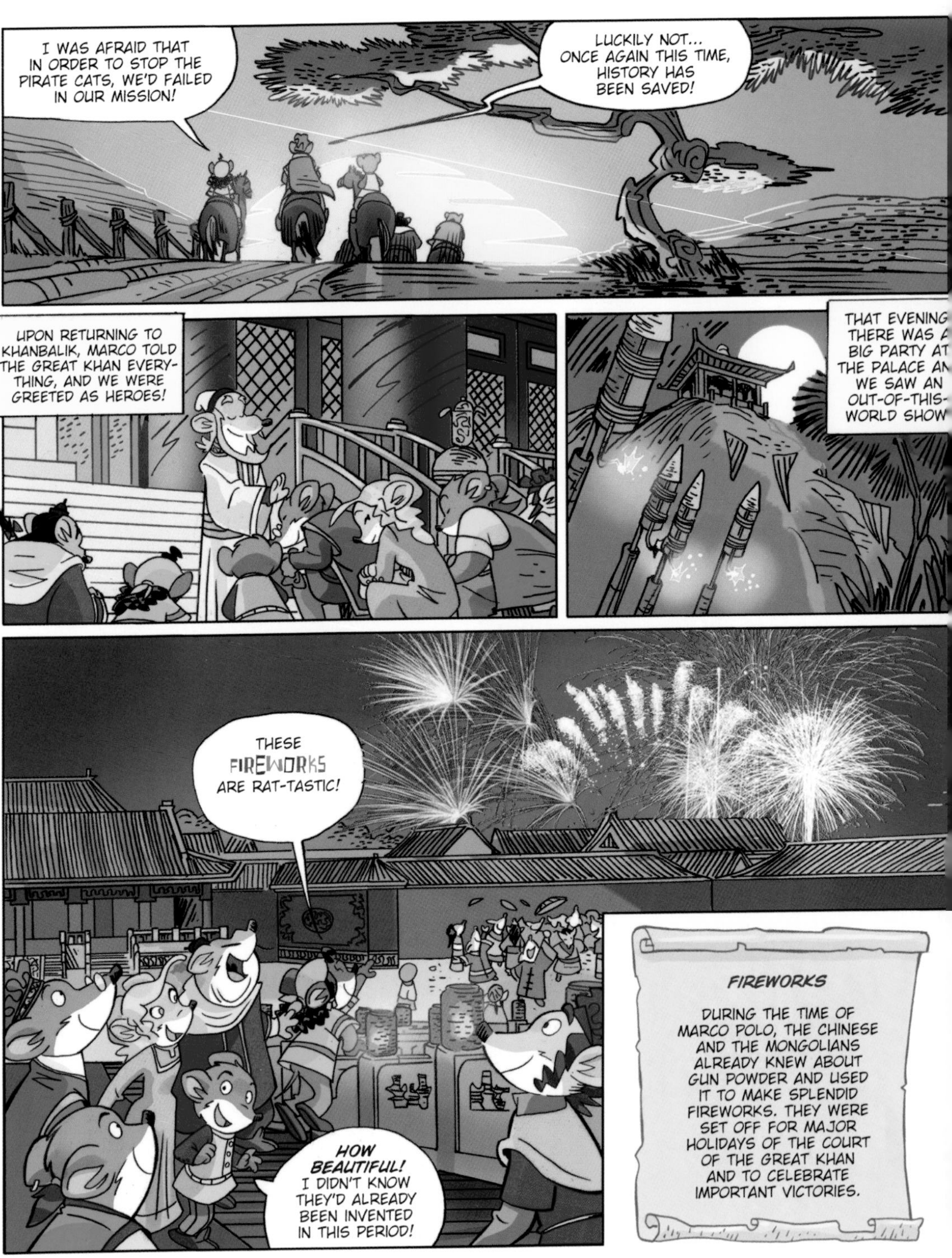

I WAS AFRAID THAT IN ORDER TO STOP THE PIRATE CATS, WE'D FAILED IN OUR MISSION!
LUCKILY NOT... ONCE AGAIN THIS TIME, HISTORY HAS BEEN SAVED!
UPON RETURNING TO KHANBALIK, MARCO TOLD THE GREAT KHAN EVERYTHING, AND WE WERE GREETED AS HEROES!
THAT EVENING THERE WAS A BIG PARTY AT THE PALACE AN WE SAW AN OUT-OF-THIS-WORLD SHOW
THESE FIREWORKS ARE RAT-TASTIC!
HOW BEAUTIFUL! I DIDN'T KNOW THEY'D ALREADY BEEN INVENTED IN THIS PERIOD!
FIREWORKS
DURING THE TIME OF MARCO POLO, THE CHINESE AND THE MONGOLIANS ALREADY KNEW ABOUT GUN POWDER AND USED IT TO MAKE SPLENDID FIREWORKS. THEY WERE SET OFF FOR MAJOR HOLIDAYS OF THE COURT OF THE GREAT KHAN AND TO CELEBRATE IMPORTANT VICTORIES.

THE NEXT DAY, WE SAID GOODBYE TO OUR FRIENDS AND RETURNED TO THE SPEEDRAT!

JUST AS THE POLOS HAD MISSED VENICE, WE, TOO, HAD REALLY MISSED OUR HOME! SO WE FINALLY ARRIVED AT PROFESSOR VON VOLT'S LAB...

FRIENDS! YOU'RE FINALLY HERE AGAIN! WELCOME BACK!

PROFESSOR VON VOLT! IT'S GREAT TO SEE YOU AGAIN!

FROM YOUR SMILES, I GATHER THAT THE MISSION WAS A SUCCESS, RIGHT?

YES, INDEED...

THE PIRATE CATS WANTED TO STEAL MARCO POLO'S DIARY AND PUBLISH IT IN HIS PLACE, BUT WE MANAGED TO FOIL THEIR **TREACHEROUS** PLAN!

DID THEY ACTUALLY WANT TO DO SOMETHING LIKE THAT? THOSE CATS REALLY ARE *SCOUNDRELS!*

TELL ME ALL THE DETAILS LATER! BUT NOW LET'S SIT DOWN AND HAVE SOMETHING TO EAT... I IMAGINE THE JOURNEY MADE YOU HUNGRY!

I'M AS HUNGRY AS A CAT!

I'M GLAD TO SEE THAT YOUR COUSIN DIGESTED MY EARPHONES COMPLETELY!

UM... THAT'S RIGHT!

ANYHOW, WHILE YOU WERE AWAY, I ALREADY TOOK CARE OF MAKING MORE SPARES!

AND WHERE DID YOU PUT THEM, PROFESSOR?

WHERE? WELL, I PUT THEM ON...

OH, NO! HE ATE THEM AGAIN!

~BURP!~

HA, HA, HA, HA, HA, HA!

MY DEAR RODENT FRIENDS, FAREWELL UNTIL THE NEXT ADVENTURE... ANOTHER WHISKERFUL OF AN ADVENTURE, WRITTEN BY STILTON...

Geronimo Stilton!

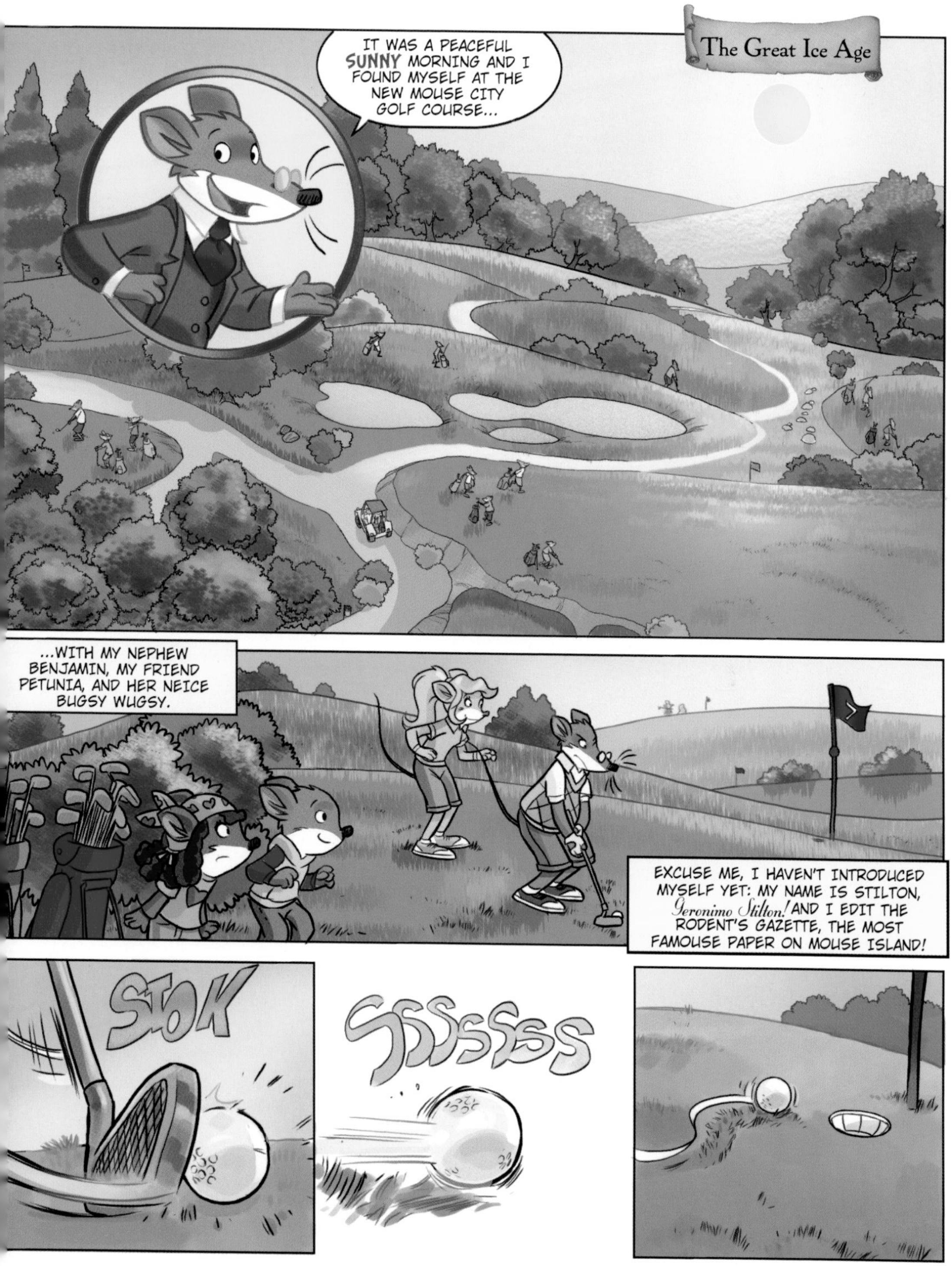
The Great Ice Age
IT WAS A PEACEFUL SUNNY MORNING AND I FOUND MYSELF AT THE NEW MOUSE CITY GOLF COURSE...
...WITH MY NEPHEW BENJAMIN, MY FRIEND PETUNIA, AND HER NEICE BUGSY WUGSY.
EXCUSE ME, I HAVEN'T INTRODUCED MYSELF YET: MY NAME IS STILTON, Geronimo Stilton! AND I EDIT THE RODENT'S GAZETTE, THE MOST FAMOUSE PAPER ON MOUSE ISLAND!
STOK
SSSSSSS

DON'T BOTHER TAK-ING IT, GERONIMO. YOU CAN SEE THE NEXT SHOT WILL BE BETTER!

YOU'RE SO NICE, PETUNIA!

YOU KNOW, I'VE WANTED TO SPEND A BIT OF TIME WITH YOU FOR SO LONG...

...WELL, HERE...WHAT I WANT TO SAY IS THAT WHEN WE'RE TOGETHER, I...

WAKE UP, GRANDSON!!!!

SQUEEEAK!

GRANDPA WILLIAM?!? WHAT ARE YOU DOING HERE?

I'M PLAYING WITH MY FRIEND, LONGSHOT PUTTER, DIRECTOR OF THE NEW MOUSE CITY SUBWAY!

GOOD MORNING!

HELLO, GERONIMO.

BUT YOU, HOWEVER, WHY AREN'T YOU AT WORK?

WELL, HERE'S...

WHEN I RAN THE PAPER, I WOULD NEVER HAVE DREAMED OF TAKING A DAY OFF, NEVER!

BUT GRANDPA, TODAY'S SUNDAY, SO I THOUGHT I'D...

I KNOW PERFECTLY WELL WHAT DAY IT IS, JUST LIKE I KNOW PERFECTLY WELL THAT YOU'RE A LAZYPAWS!

ENJOY YOUR GAME, BUT I WANT AN ARTICLE ON GOLF TOMORROW!

→SIGH!← I'VE GOT A FEELING I'M DONE RELAXING FOR TODAY!

WHEN GRANDPA WILLIAM HAD GONE AWAY...

WONDERFUL SHOT, UNCLE!

THE BALL SOARED AWAY AS FAR AS THE EYE CAN SEE!

A LITTLE TOO FAR! I'M NOT SURE I KNOW WHICH DIRECTION IT WENT!

SQUEEEAK!

OOPS! SORRY, COUSIN, I GAUGED THE TRAJECTORY OF MY SHOT BADLY!

TRAP!?!

I DIDN'T KNOW YOU LIKED TO PLAY GOLF!

I DON'T JUST LIKE IT: I'M A CHAMPION!

THE SECRET TO GOLF IS TO PLACE THE BALL ON THE GROUND WELL...

...AND THEN HIT IT WITH ALL THE POWER YOU'VE GOT!

SWIIISSSHH

SPLAFF

GERONIMO, ARE YOU OKAY?

UM...YES...

SEE, COUSIN? I'M A REAL CHAMPION!

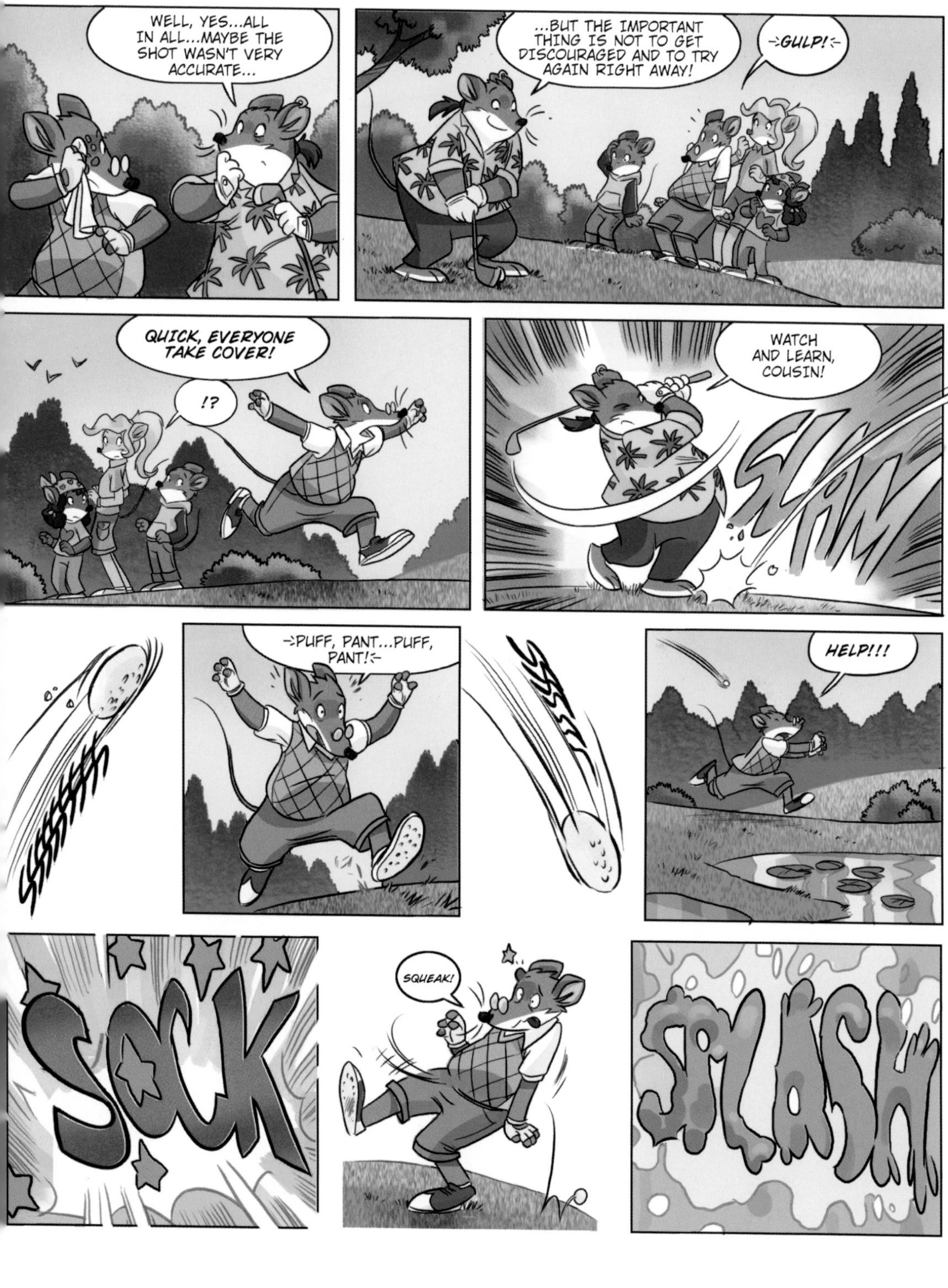

WELL, YES...ALL IN ALL...MAYBE THE SHOT WASN'T VERY ACCURATE...
...BUT THE IMPORTANT THING IS NOT TO GET DISCOURAGED AND TO TRY AGAIN RIGHT AWAY!
GULP!
QUICK, EVERYONE TAKE COVER!
!?
WATCH AND LEARN, COUSIN!
SLAM
SSSSSSSS
PUFF, PANT...PUFF, PANT!
SSSSS
HELP!!!
SOCK
SQUEAK!
SPLASH

POOR ME, I REALLY WOULD'VE BEEN BETTER OFF GOING TO THE OFFICE TODAY!

RIBBIT, RIBBIT, RIBBIT!

UM...COULD YOU GET OFF MY HEAD?

BUT OF COURSE, GERONIMO!

MOLDY MOZZARELLA! A TALKING FROG?!

THIS FROG IS ACTUALLY A LITTLE ROBOT!

B-B-BUT...THAT VOICE... PROFESSOR VON VOLT, IS THAT YOU?

INDEED, IT IS! THIS FROG IS MY LATEST INVENTION. PRETTY NICE, DON'T YOU THINK? I MANAGED TO TRACK YOU DOWN WITH IT.

I NEED TO SEE YOU AND YOUR FRIENDS...HISTORY IS IN DANGER!

-‹GULP!›- IF THAT'S THE CASE, PROFESSOR, WE'LL BE **RIGHT THERE!**

A HALF HOUR LATER, WE WERE IN PETUNIA'S SUV, FOLLOWING THE FROG ROBOT'S DIRECTIONS...

AT THE NEXT LIGHT, TURN RIGHT!

...WHICH QUICKLY TOOK US TO PROF. VON VOLT'S SECRET LAB!

HELLO, PROFESSOR! TELL US EVERYTHING!

ARE THE **PIRATE CATS** BEHIND THIS?

UNFORTUNATELY, YES, GERONIMO. YOU GUESSED RIGHT!

THE TEMPOGRAPH--THE DEVICE I CREATED TO KEEP TRACK OF HISTORY--SHOWS THEY ARE TRAVELING INTO THE PAST AGAIN!

AND WHERE ARE THEY HEADED THIS TIME? HAVE YOU FIGURED IT OUT YET, PROFESSOR?

THAT'S THE STRANGE THING: THEIR DESTINATION IS THE NEANDER VALLEY IN GERMANY, AROUND 40,000 YEARS AGO!

40,000 YEARS AGO? BUT THAT WAS DURING THE **PLEISTOCENE!**

PLEISTOCENE

IN THIS GEOLOGICAL ERA (1,800,000-11,000 YEARS AGO) THE EARTH LOOKED A LOT DIFFERENT FROM TODAY. AS A MATTER OF FACT, THE PLEISTOCENE WAS CHARACTERIZED BY THE CLIMATE CONSTANTLY GETTING COLDER, WHICH CAUSED THE NORTH POLE ICE SHEET AND GLACIERS FROM THE MOUNTAINS TO INVADE MOST OF NORTH AMERICA AND EUROPE. THIS PHENOMENON IS KNOWN AS GLACIATION AND WAS THE START OF THE ICE AGE. THE AREAS SHELTERED FROM ICE, LIKE THE NEANDER VALLEY (NEANDERTHAL) IN NORTHERN GERMANY, WERE FILLED WITH GRASSLANDS AND FORESTS IN WHICH MANY SPECIES OF WILD ANIMALS (DEER, BEAR, WOLVES, MARMOTS, AND MAMMOTHS) AND THE ANCESTORS OF MODERN HUMANS LIVED.

IF I'M NOT WRONG, THERE WEREN'T ANY CITIES IN THIS ERA, ONLY FORESTS!

YES, THAT'S RIGHT! AND WIDE GRASSLANDS, TOO!

HMM...A PERFECT PLACE TO PLAY GOLF! HOW NICE!

HMPH, TRAP...HOW CAN YOU THINK OF PLAYING RIGHT NOW?

BETTER YET, DO YOU HAVE ANY IDEA WHAT THE PIRATE CATS' GOAL COULD BE?

NO, NO IDEA AT ALL!

THE AREA BORDERED BY THE ICE SHEET WAS PRACTICALLY UNINHABITED, EXCEPT FOR...EARLY NEANDERTHALS!

EARLY NEANDERTHALS

LIVED BETWEEN 100,000 AND 30,000 YEARS AGO. THEIR NAME COMES FROM THE FACT THAT IN 1856, SOME OF THEIR REMAINS WERE FOUND IN A CAVE IN THE NEANDER VALLEY. COMPARED TO MODERN HUMANS (HOMO SAPIENS), NEANDERTHALS WERE SHORTER AND HAD SHORTER ARMS AND LEGS. THEIR TYPICAL FACIAL FEATURES WERE A LOW, FLAT SKULL, PRONOUNCED CHEEKBONES, AND A RECEDING CHIN.

WHATEVER THOSE CRUMMY CATS MAY HAVE IN MIND, WE'VE GOT TO LEAVE RIGHT AWAY!

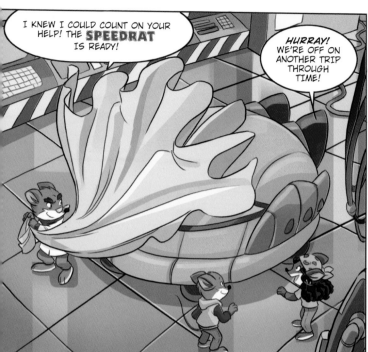

I KNEW I COULD COUNT ON YOUR HELP! THE **SPEEDRAT** IS READY!

HURRAY! WE'RE OFF ON ANOTHER TRIP THROUGH TIME!

I'M GIVING YOU MY SPECIAL EARPHONES THAT LET YOU SPEAK AND UNDERSTAND THE LANGUAGE OF THE TIME!

I'LL PUT MY GOLF BAG NEXT TO THE CLOTHES WE'LL WEAR WHEN WE GET THERE!

PLEASE KEEP THE PIRATE CATS FROM CHANGING HISTORY TO BENEFIT THEMSELVES!

DON'T WORRY, PROFESSOR, WE'LL STOP THEM!

TAKE-OFFFF!!!

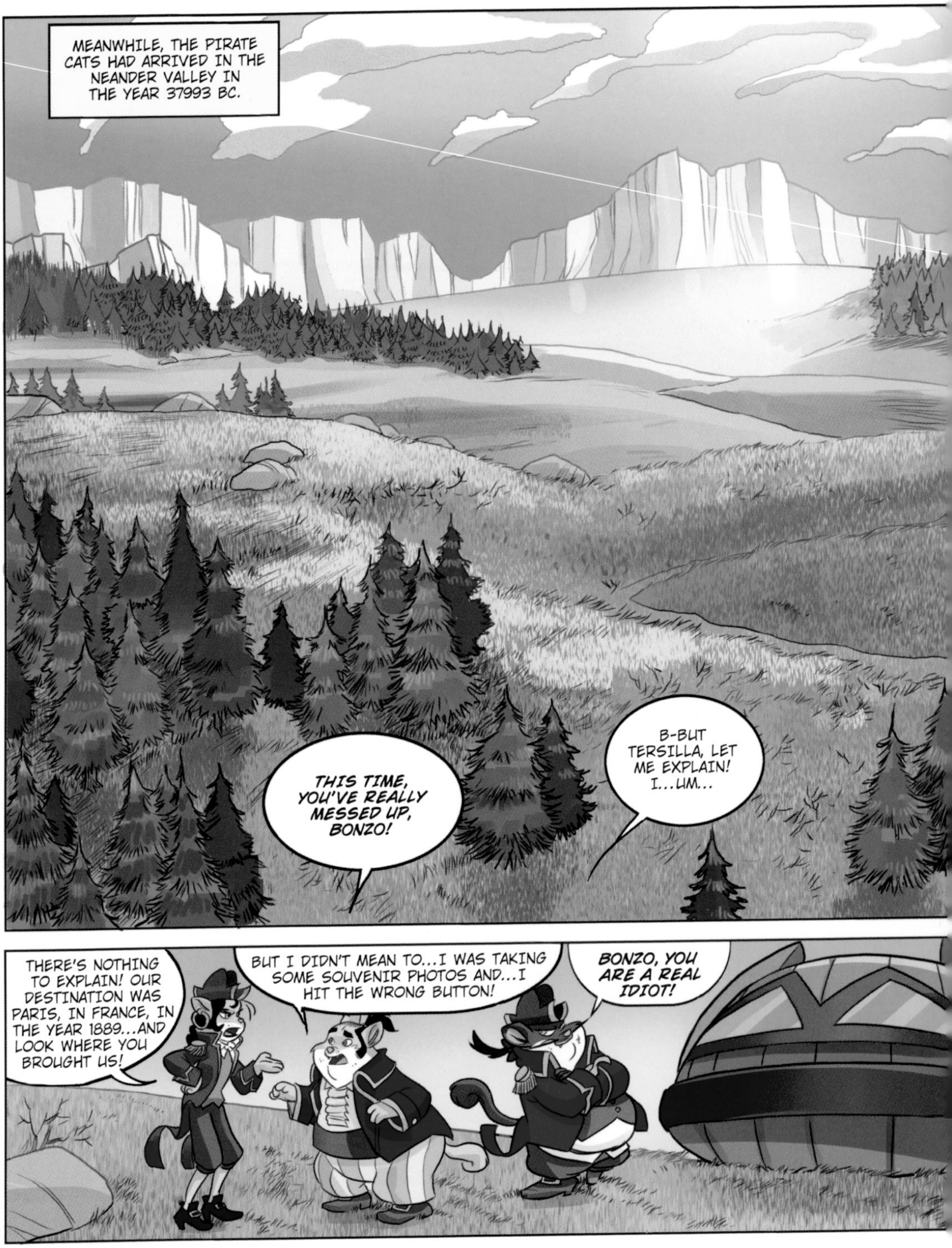
MEANWHILE, THE PIRATE CATS HAD ARRIVED IN THE NEANDER VALLEY IN THE YEAR 37993 BC.
THIS TIME, YOU'VE REALLY MESSED UP, BONZO!
B-BUT TERSILLA, LET ME EXPLAIN! I...UM...
THERE'S NOTHING TO EXPLAIN! OUR DESTINATION WAS PARIS, IN FRANCE, IN THE YEAR 1889...AND LOOK WHERE YOU BROUGHT US!
BUT I DIDN'T MEAN TO...I WAS TAKING SOME SOUVENIR PHOTOS AND...I HIT THE WRONG BUTTON!
BONZO, YOU ARE A REAL IDIOT!

CAN'T WE REVERSE COURSE AND GO TO PARIS NOW?

NO, DADDY DEAR... THE CATJET ONLY HAS ENOUGH FUEL TO TAKE US BACK TO OUR OWN TIME!

I DON'T CARE ABOUT SOME PHOTO! WE WERE SUPPOSED TO BE STEALING THE EIFFEL TOWER ON THE DAY IT WAS INAUGURATED!

WELL, SINCE WE'RE ALREADY HERE NOW, HOW ABOUT I TAKE A **PHOTO?**

WOULD YOU KNOCK IT OFF, YOU PAIN IN THE TAIL!*

*PAIN IN THE NECK

~GULP!~

SOMEONE'S **ATTACKING US!**

HURRY UP, EVERYBODY ON BOARD! WE'VE GOT TO TAKE OFF AGAIN!

61

FSHUOOOOAA

CRASH

YOU JUST GET DUMBER AND DUMBER, BONZO!

WHAT'VE YOU DONE?!

MEOW DOWN*, DADDY DEAR! WE HAVE TO BE CAREFUL ABOUT HOW WE ACT!

A THOUSAND TUMBLING TABBY CATS! CAVE PEOPLE!

*CALM DOWN

DID YOU NOTICE? THEY DON'T LOOK LIKE THEY'RE AFRAID OF US!

IT'S PROBABLY BECAUSE THEY'VE NEVER SEEN ANY CATS BEFORE IN THEIR LIVES!

THEY'RE ARMED. WHAT DO WE DO NOW?

TOOLS

NEANDERTHALS HADN'T DISCOVERED IRON AND MADE THEIR TOOLS OUT OF WOOD, BONE, OR STONE. THEY ALSO USED FLINT--A SPECIAL KIND OF ROCK WITH CHARACTERISTICS LIKE GLASS THAT WHEN SPLINTERED OFF, PROVIDED A SHARPENED FOIL THAT WAS USED A GREAT DEAL TO MAKE WEAPONS (KNIVES, SPEARS, AND AXES) AND OTHER TOOLS OF VARIOUS SHAPES AND DIMENSIONS TO WORK WOOD, SCRAPE ANIMAL SKINS, AND CARVE MEAT.

WELL, WE CAN TAKE A BEAUTIFUL PHOTO!

?!?

CLICK

SQUEEEAK!!!

DID YOU SEE THE FLASH OF LIGHTNING?

YES, THE FLASH OF LIGHTNING! I SAW IT!

THEY ARE GODS FROM THE HEAVENS!

BOW DOWN BEFORE THE GODS OF LIGHTNING!

FORGIVE US FOR ATTACKING YOU, OH, POWERFUL GODS! I, RAT-KUN, AND ALL THE RODENTS OF MY TRIBE ARE AT YOUR SERVICE!

POWERFUL GODS? I THOUGHT WE WERE PIRATE CATS!

SILENCE, HAIRBALL!

THE CAVE PEOPLE MISTOOK THE CAMERA FLASH FOR LIGHTNING!

COME ON! COME WITH ME! I'VE GOT AN IDEA!

BUT...BUT...COME WHERE? AND DO WHAT?

DO WHAT? SIMPLE: PLAY THE ROLE OF GODS! HEE, HEE, HEE!

I GRANT YOU PERMISSION TO GET UP, RAT-KUN!

TH-THANK YOU...

YOU KNOW WE NORMALLY WOULD HAVE ALREADY PUNISHED YOU FOR YOUR ATTACK BY INCINERATING YOU WITH LIGHTNING!

-GULP-

BUT WE FEEL GENEROUS TODAY AND HAVE DECIDED TO SPARE YOU!

TH-TH-THANK YOU... AND OUR APOLOGIES, ONCE AGAIN!

FROM A DISTANCE, SOME OF MY COMPANIONS CONFUSED THE STRANGE ANIMAL YOU TRAVEL ON WITH THE ICE GIANT!

THE ICE GIANT?!?

EXPLAIN THAT TO US, RAT-KUN! WHAT IS THIS MYSTERIOUS ICE GIANT?

IT'S A HUGE, HORRIBLE CREATURE...IT'S FIVE TIMES BIGGER THAN A MAMMOTH AND HAS ENORMOUS TUSKS!

THE MAMMOTH

THE MAMMOTH IS A SPECIES OF ELEPHANT THAT LIVED FROM ABOUT 5,000,000 TO 6,000 YEARS AGO IN EUROPE, AFRICA, AND NORTH AMERICA. COMPARED TO TODAY'S ELEPHANTS, MAMMOTHS HAD LONG, CURVED TUSKS AND THICK FUR ALL OVER THEIR BODIES. THEY AVERAGED AROUND 9.2 FEET TALL AND COULD REACH 14.7 FEET IN LENGTH. LIKE TODAY'S ELEPHANTS, MAMMOTHS WERE HERBIVORES.

IN THE PAST FEW DAYS, THE RODENTS OF MY TRIBE HAVE OFTEN HEARD **FEARSOME WAILS...**

"...THAT CAME FROM THE LARGE ICE SHEET. AND WHEN THEY APPROACHED IT, THEY SAW A HORRIBLE MONSTER!"

NOW WE'RE SO SCARED WE DON'T DARE VENTURE OVER THERE ANYMORE!

HMM...VERY INTERESTING...

DID YOU HEAR THAT? MAYBE OUR TRIP WASN'T A TOTAL WASTE!

WHAT DO YOU MEAN, TERSILLA?

IF WE MANAGE TO CAPTURE THE ICE GIANT AND BRING IT BACK TO CATBURG WITH US, WE'LL BE FAMOUS!

YOU WANT...TO CAPTURE THAT **monster?!?**

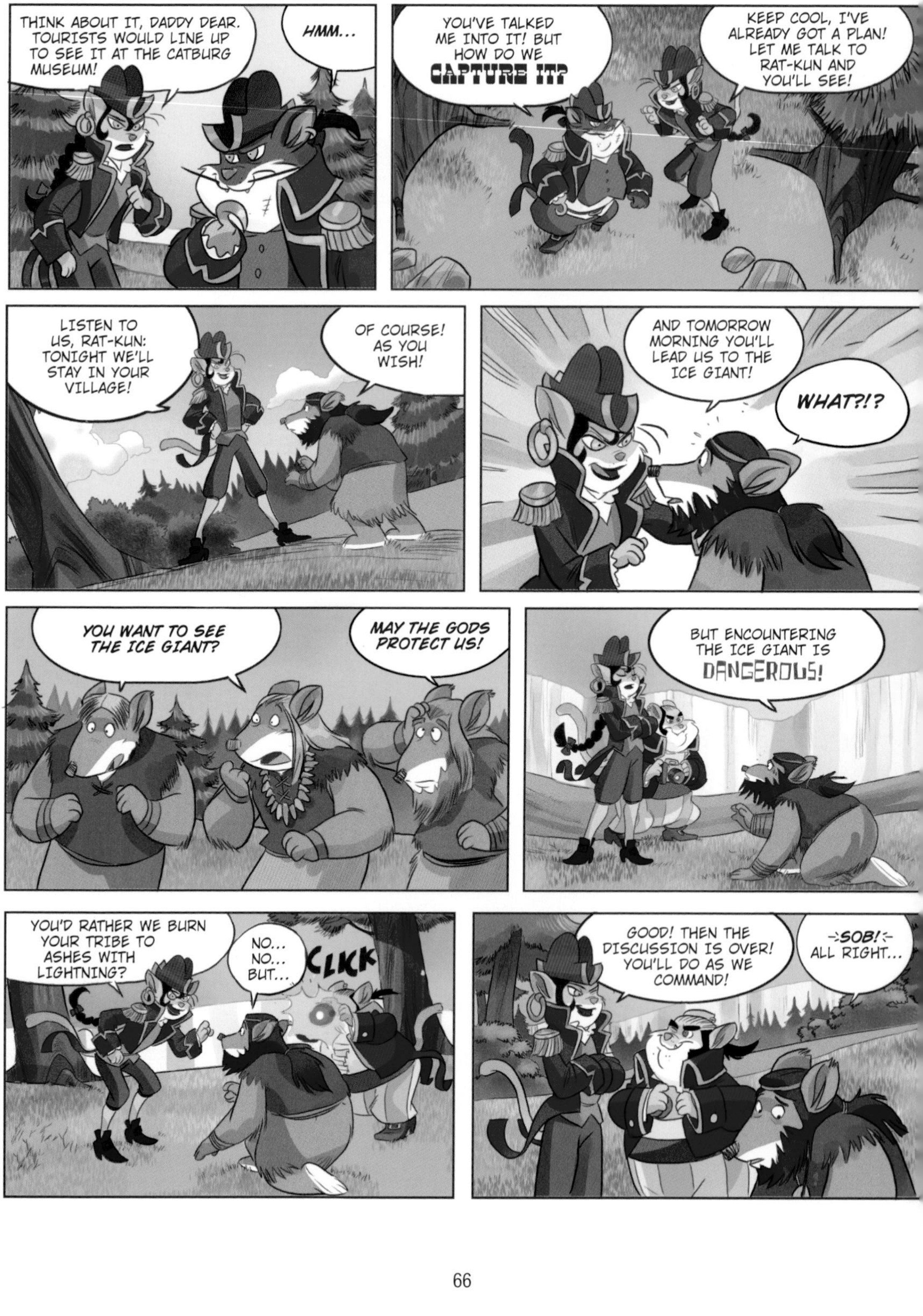
THINK ABOUT IT, DADDY DEAR. TOURISTS WOULD LINE UP TO SEE IT AT THE CATBURG MUSEUM!
HMM...
YOU'VE TALKED ME INTO IT! BUT HOW DO WE CAPTURE IT?
KEEP COOL, I'VE ALREADY GOT A PLAN! LET ME TALK TO RAT-KUN AND YOU'LL SEE!
LISTEN TO US, RAT-KUN: TONIGHT WE'LL STAY IN YOUR VILLAGE!
OF COURSE! AS YOU WISH!
AND TOMORROW MORNING YOU'LL LEAD US TO THE ICE GIANT!
WHAT?!?
YOU WANT TO SEE THE ICE GIANT?
MAY THE GODS PROTECT US!
BUT ENCOUNTERING THE ICE GIANT IS DANGEROUS!
YOU'D RATHER WE BURN YOUR TRIBE TO ASHES WITH LIGHTNING?
NO... NO... BUT...
CLCK
GOOD! THEN THE DISCUSSION IS OVER! YOU'LL DO AS WE COMMAND!
SOB! ALL RIGHT...

MEANWHILE, WE'D LANDED THE SPEEDRAT RIGHT ON THE ICE SHEET...

BRRR... IT'S COLD AS A CAT'S HEART.

WELL, WE'RE RIGHT IN THE MIDDLE OF THE **WURM GLACIATION!**

THE WURM GLACIATION

WAS THE LAST BIG GLACIATION TO AFFECT THE EARTH. IT LASTED FROM AROUND 80,000 TO 11,000 YEARS AGO AND GETS ITS NAME FROM A RIVER IN THE REGION OF BAVARIA, IN GERMANY. IT'S ALSO KNOWN AS THE WISCONSIN (FROM THE NAME OF THE STATE IN NORTH AMERICA) OR WEICHSEL GLACIATION (THE NAME OF A REGION IN NORTHERN EUROPE).

I KNOW, BUT I WONDER HOW ICE AGE CAVE PEOPLE KEPT FROM FREEZING **DRESSED** LIKE THIS!

CLOTHES

NEANDERTHALS WERE PROBABLY THE FIRST HUMAN BEINGS WHO REGULARLY WORE CLOTHING TO PROTECT THEMSELVES FROM THE COLD. THEIR CLOTHING WAS MADE FROM THE SKINS AND FURS OF VARIOUS ANIMALS, WHICH, AFTER BEING STRETCHED AND SCRAPED WITH FLINT TOOLS, WERE SEWN INTO CLOTHING AND SHOES. NEANDERTHALS MADE NECKLACES AND BRACELETS FROM ANIMAL TEETH TO WEAR AS JEWELRY.

NOW WE CAN GO! HEY, WAIT A MINUTE...TRAP, WHAT ARE YOU DOING HERE WITH THAT GOLF BAG?

TO STAY ON TOP OF HIS GAME, A CHAMPION MUST NEVER STOP TRAINING!

BUT GOLF HADN'T BEEN INVENTED YET IN THIS ERA! YOU CAN'T CARRY GOLF EQUIPMENT!

COME ON, COUSIN, I PROMISE I'LL ONLY PLAY AFTER THE MISSION IS ACCOMPLISHED!

ALL RIGHT, ALL RIGHT...IT'S USELESS TO ARGUE ABOUT IT!

BUT WHERE SHOULD WE START LOOKING FOR THE PIRATE CATS?

THERE'S ONLY ICE AROUND HERE!

THE ICE SHEET SEEMS TO END OVER THERE! LET'S TRY TO TAKE A LOOK!

LOOK! THERE'S A FOREST OVER THERE! WHAT A *RAT-TASTIC* VIEW!

YOU'RE A REGULAR ROMAN-TIC, COUSIN!

SQUEEEAK!

I'M FALLINGGGGGGG!

TUMF

68

GERONIMO, ARE YOU OKAY?

YES! LUCKILY I LANDED ON A BIG, HAIRY CUSHION!

UMM...MAYBE YOU'D BETTER TAKE A CLOSER LOOK, UNCLE!

MOLDY MOZZARELLA! I'M ON THE BACK OF A MAMMOTH!

BAAARR FRRR

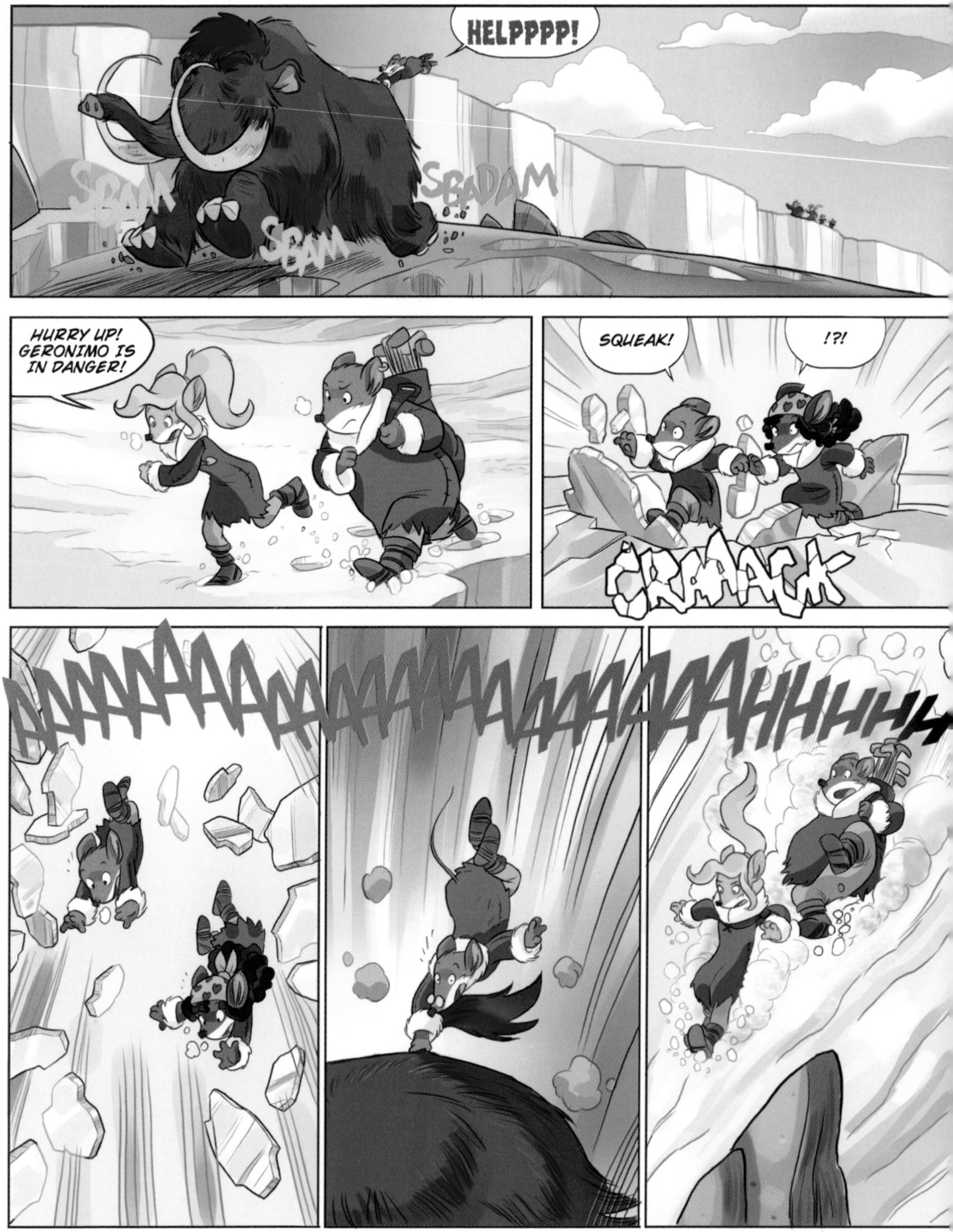
HELPPPP!
SBAM
SBADAM
SBAM
HURRY UP! GERONIMO IS IN DANGER!
SQUEAK!
!?!
CRAAACK
AAAAAAAAAAAAAAAAAAAAAAAAAAAAHHHHH

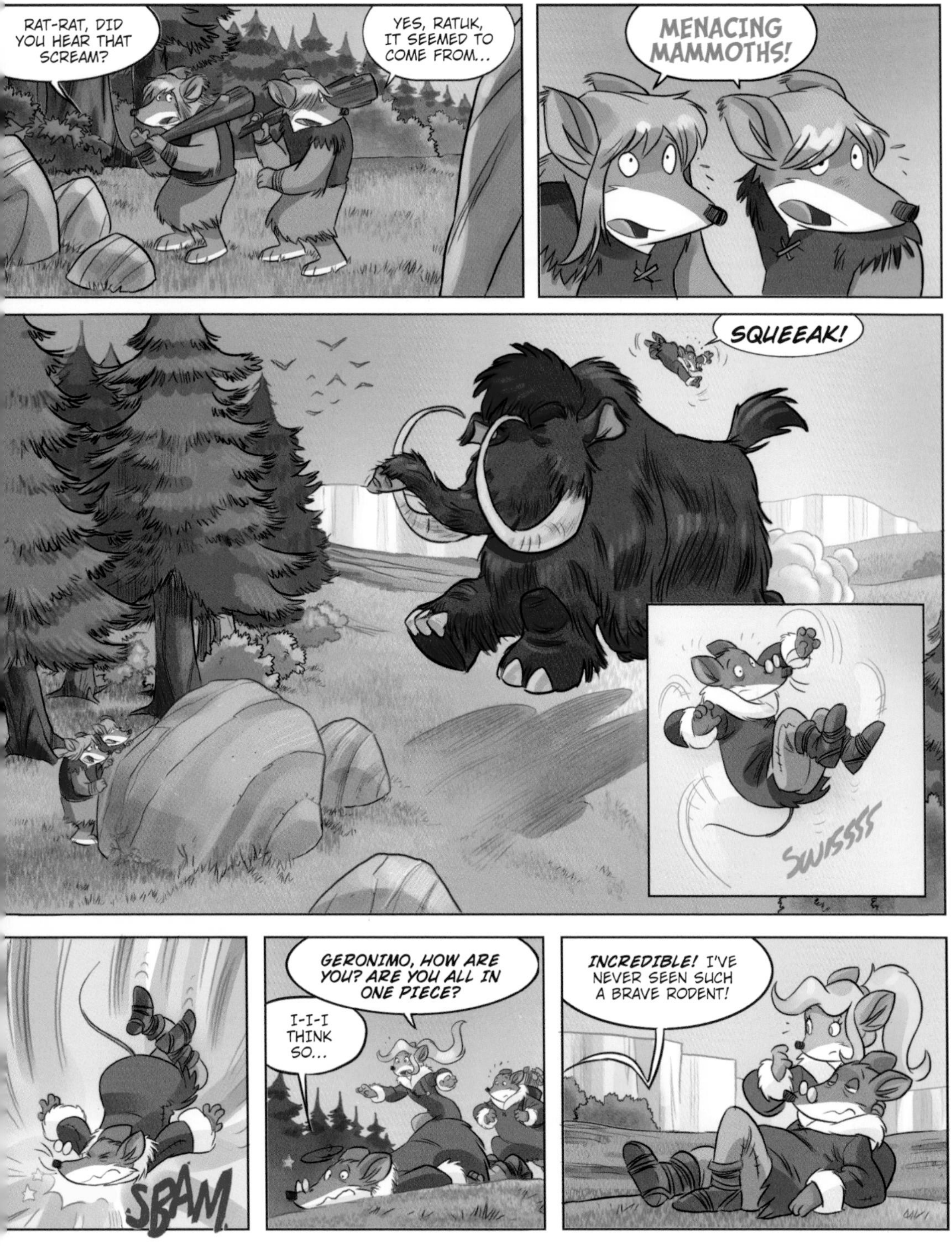
RAT-RAT, DID YOU HEAR THAT SCREAM?
YES, RATUK, IT SEEMED TO COME FROM...
MENACING MAMMOTHS!
SQUEEAK!
SWISSSS
SBAM
GERONIMO, HOW ARE YOU? ARE YOU ALL IN ONE PIECE?
I-I-I THINK SO...
INCREDIBLE! I'VE NEVER SEEN SUCH A BRAVE RODENT!

NO ONE IN OUR TRIBE WOULD HAVE EVER DARED TO FACE THAT MAMMOTH!

THEY ALL KNOW IT'S A VERY FEROCIOUS BEAST!

WH-WH-WHAT? DID YOU SAY FEROCIOUS?

IN THE LAST FEW DAYS, IT'S GONE AFTER ANYBODY WHO CAME NEAR IT...WHEN IT WASN'T EVEN BEING ATTACKED!

I THINK IT'S EVEN SCARIER THAN THE ICE GIANT!

WHAT ARE YOU TALKING ABOUT? THIS IS JUST A MAMMOTH, WHILE THE ICE GIANT...

...IS A REAL MONSTER!

I THINK THE MAMMOTH IS MUCH WORSE!

NO WAY!

UM... EXCUSE ME?

EXCUSE ME FOR BUTTING IN, BUT...COULD YOU TELL US WHO YOU ARE?

OH, YEAH, SORRY! MY NAME IS RAT-RAT...

...AND I'M RATUK! WE'RE THE CHILDREN OF THE GREAT TRIBAL LEADER RAT-KUN!

PLEASED TO MEET YOU! MY NAME IS STILTONUT, GERONIMUT STILTONUT. THIS IS MY FRIEND PETTUT, MY COUSIN TRAPPUT, MY NEPHEW, BEN--!

BUT... WHERE...?

MOLDY MOZZARELLA! WHAT HAPPENED TO BENJAMUT AND BUGSORUT?

I DON'T UNDER-STAND...THEY WERE RIGHT BEHIND US!

THAT'S RIGHT...HOW DID THEY GET LOST?

IF THEY GOT LOST, IT WON'T BE EASY TO FIND THEM: THE REGION IS HUGE!

BUT WE HAVE TO FIND THEM!

COME TO THE VILLAGE! WE'LL GET ALL THE RODENTS TOGETHER AND SEARCH THE GRASSLANDS!

BUT...

RATUK AND RAT-RAT ARE RIGHT! WE DON'T KNOW THE AREA AND WE'LL RISK GETTING OURSELVES LOST, TOO!

THAT'S TRUE...LET'S GO!

CHEER UP, GERONIMO! I'M SURE...

"...THAT BENJAMIN AND BUGSY ARE OKAY!"

A LITTLE LATER, WE ARRIVED IN A GENUINE PRIMITIVE VILLAGE...

~SLURP!~ THIS LOOKS GREAT!

GET A MOVE ON, TRAPPUT!

DWELLINGS

NEANDERTHALS LIVED IN CAVES OR CAMPS OUTDOORS, WHERE THEY BUILT HUTS OUT OF ANIMAL SKINS STRETCHED OVER A PANELWORK OF STAKES OR MAMMOTH BONES. TO WARM UP, KEEP WILD ANIMALS AWAY, AND COOK, THEY USED FIRE, WHICH THEY LIT BY RUBBING TWO STONES OR STICKS TOGETHER.

FOOD

THE NEANDERTHAL DIET MOSTLY CONSISTED OF THE MEAT OF THE ANIMALS THEY HUNTED AND FRUIT AND ROOTS THEY GATHERED IN FORESTS. DEER, HARES, MAMMOTHS, MARMOTS, BEARS, AND REINDEER WERE THE REGULAR PREY THEY HUNTED. THEY THEN USED THE BONES AND SKIN AS WELL TO MAKE CLOTHING, HUTS, AND VARIOUS TOOLS.

YOUR **TRIBE** SEEMS VERY BUSY!

OH, YES! THIS EVENING WE'RE HOSTING A BIG BANQUET IN HONOR OF THREE POWERFUL GODS WHO ARRIVED TODAY!

THREE GODS?

UM...DO YOU SMELL THE STINK OF THE PIRATE CATS, TOO?

THE P-P-PIRATE CATS!

THAT'S RIGHT! WITH BENJAMIN AND BUGSY DISAPPEARING, I ALMOST FORGOT ABOUT THEM!

OUR FATHER'S OVER THERE: HE'S WITH THE GODS!

UH-OH! I SINCERELY HOPE THEY AREN'T...

...THE PIRATE CATS!!!

GERONIMO STILTON AND HIS FRIENDS?

75

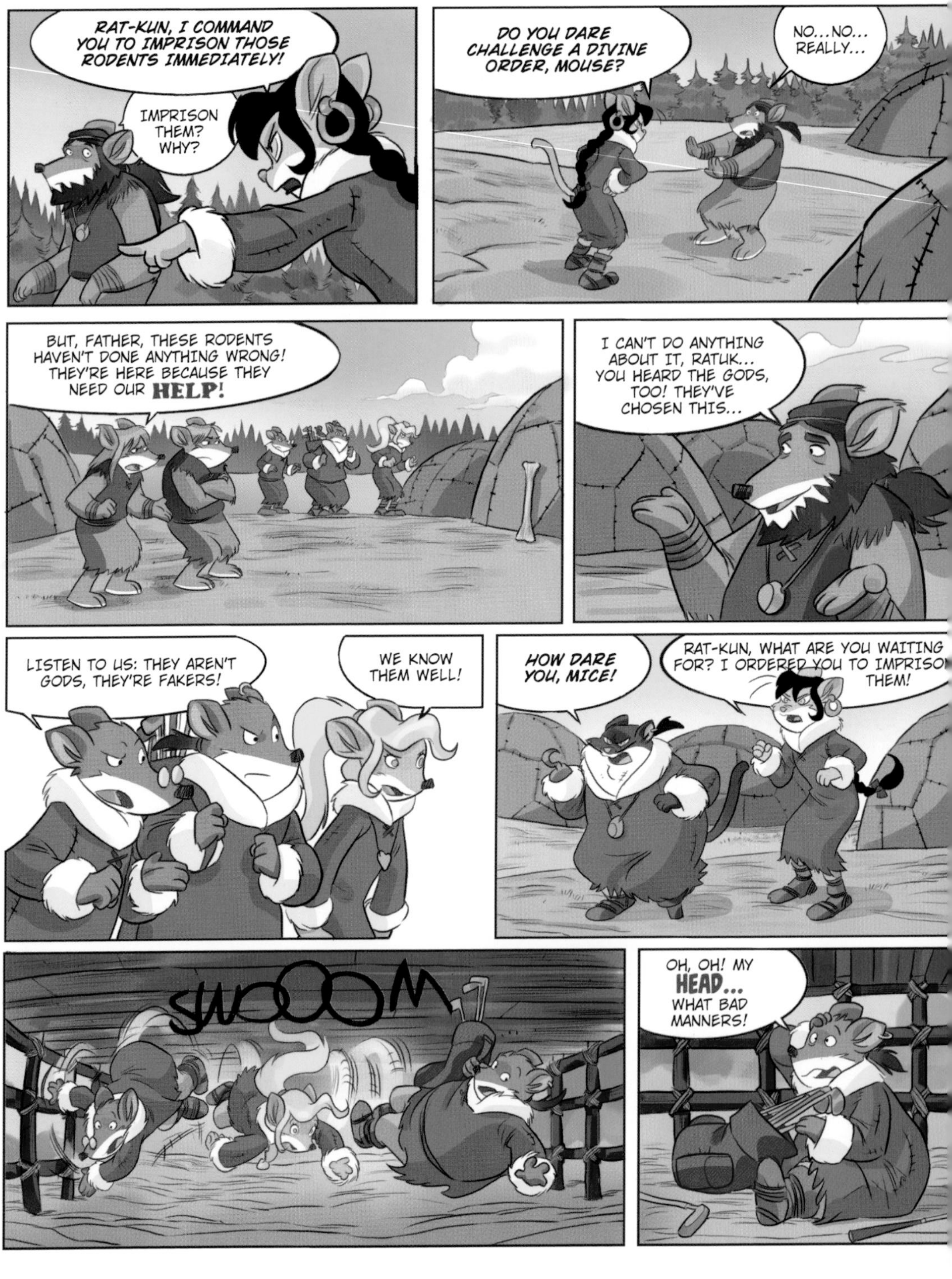
RAT-KUN, I COMMAND YOU TO IMPRISON THOSE RODENTS IMMEDIATELY!
IMPRISON THEM? WHY?
DO YOU DARE CHALLENGE A DIVINE ORDER, MOUSE?
NO...NO... REALLY...
BUT, FATHER, THESE RODENTS HAVEN'T DONE ANYTHING WRONG! THEY'RE HERE BECAUSE THEY NEED OUR HELP!
I CAN'T DO ANYTHING ABOUT IT, RATUK... YOU HEARD THE GODS, TOO! THEY'VE CHOSEN THIS...
LISTEN TO US: THEY AREN'T GODS, THEY'RE FAKERS!
WE KNOW THEM WELL!
HOW DARE YOU, MICE!
RAT-KUN, WHAT ARE YOU WAITING FOR? I ORDERED YOU TO IMPRISO THEM!
SWOOOM
OH, OH! MY HEAD... WHAT BAD MANNERS!

I BEG YOU TO FREE US! OUR NIECE AND NEPHEW ARE IN GRAVE DANGER...AND SO ARE YOU!

SORRY, GERONIMUT, BUT WE CAN'T DISOBEY THE GODS...FOR THE SAKE OF OUR *FUR!*

HOW CAN WE GET IT ACROSS TO YOU...THOSE AREN'T GODS! THEY'RE CATS AND THEY'RE SCOUNDRELS!

IT'S A WASTE OF BREATH, GERONIMO! THEY'LL NEVER BELIEVE US.

YOU'RE RIGHT. BUT ISN'T THERE SOMETHING WE CAN DO?

FOR NOW, WE CAN JUST STAY CALM AND WAIT FOR THE RIGHT OPPORTUNITY TO ESCAPE.

WHILE WE'RE WAITING, I HOPE THEY GIVE US SOME-THING TO EAT AT LEAST: I'M HUNGRY AS A FELINE!

-SIGH!-

THAT NIGHT, A BIG BANQUET WAS HELD IN HONOR OF THE PIRATE CATS.

WE GOT TO SLEEP LATE THAT NIGHT AND AT DAWN...

ZZZZZZ

SQUEEAK!

SPLASH

WAKE UP, MICE, IT'S TIME TO GO!

GO? WITH YOU? WHERE TO?

WE'RE ALL LEAVING TO HUNT THE ICE GIANT!

THAT'S THE MONSTROUS CREATURE THAT RATUK WAS TALKING ABOUT! SO IS THAT YOUR GOAL?

RIGHT! WE'RE GOING TO TAKE IT TO CATBURG WITH US AND YOU CAN'T DO ANYTHING TO STOP US!

AS A MATTER OF FACT, YOUR FATE HAS BEEN SETTLED: WE'VE ORDERED RAT-KUN TO SACRIFICE YOU TO THE ICE GIANT BY THROWING YOU INTO A **CHASM...** HEE, HEE, HEE!

-GULP!-
WHAT A
HORRIBLE
END!

WHAT A
CHEESEHEAD!

HAVE YOU PUT EVERYTHING
ONTO THE CATJET WE'LL NEED
TO CAPTURE THE MONSTER?

OF COURSE,
TERSILLA! I'VE
GOT THE BLOW-
TORCH...

...AND THE STEEL CABLES
WE WERE GOING TO
USE TO STEAL THE
EIFFEL TOWER!

PERFECT...LET'S
GET GOING!

THE EXPEDITION WENT
ACROSS THE GRASS-
LANDS, HEADING FOR
THE ICE GIANT...

79

STOP!

THE GREAT ICE SHEET IS PAST THESE TREES!

IT WOULD BE BETTER TO LEAVE THE CAGE WITH THE PRISONERS HERE! IF THE GIANT ATTACKS US, IT WILL GET IN OUR WAY!

AGREED. IN THAT CASE, LET'S SACRIFICE THE PRISONERS WHEN WE GET BACK!

FOUR RODENTS FROM MY TRIBE WILL STAY TO KEEP GUARD OVER THEM!

POOR US! HOW'RE WE GOING TO GET OUT NOW?

DON'T DESPAIR... YOU'LL SEE HOW WE GET AWAY!

I WISH I WERE AS HOPEFUL AS PETUNIA!

THE CATS WERE ABSOLUTELY DETER-MINED TO CARRY OUT THEIR PLAN...

HERE WE ARE NOW...W-W-WE'RE...

CHIN UP, RAT-KUN, WHAT'RE YOU AFRAID OF? YOU'RE IN THE COMPANY OF THREE DEITIES!

BESIDES, AT THE MOMENT THERE'RE NO MONSTERS TO BE SEEN AROUND HERE!

SQUEEEAK!!!

?!?

THE MONSTER'S ARRIVED! QUICK, RUN AWAY!

TH-TH-THERE IT IS...THAT'S IT!

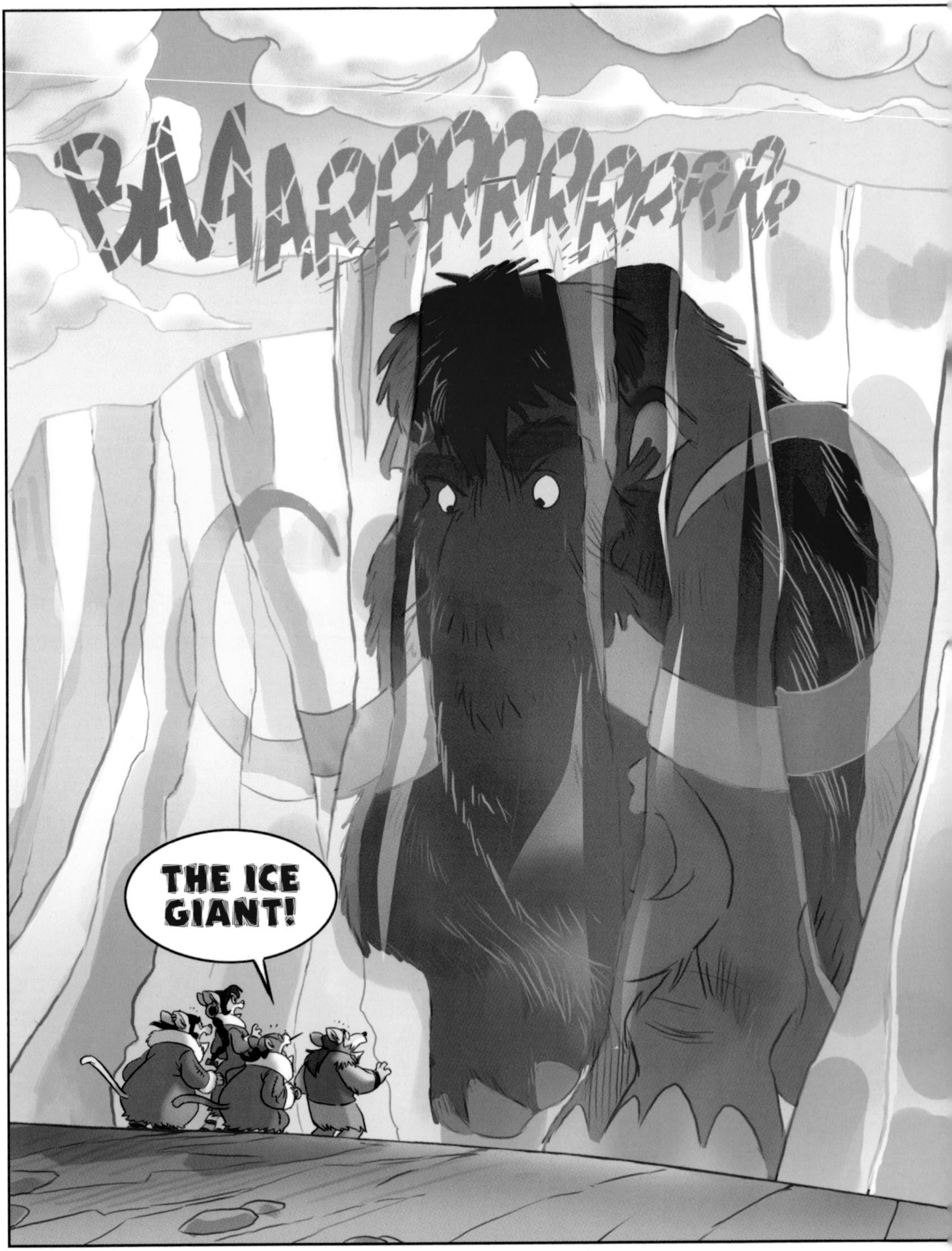
BAARRRRRRRRRRR
THE ICE GIANT!

IT'S RIGHT BEHIND THAT WALL OF ICE! BONZO, GET THE BLOWTORCH!

WAIT, TERSILLA, LOOK!

CRUNCHY CRACKERS! THE ICE GIANT HAS DISAPPEARED!

STRANGE...IT'S AS IF SOMETHING SCARED IT! BUT WHAT...

CRACK

HUH?

ROOAAARRR

MENACING MAMMOTHS!

TWO SABER-TOOTH TIGERS!

SABER-TOOTH TIGERS (OR MACHAIRODONTINAE)

WERE PART OF THE FELIDAE SUBFAMILY, WHICH ALSO INCLUDES TODAY'S CATS AND LIONS, FOR EXAMPLE. WE KNOW LITTLE ABOUT SABER-TOOTH TIGERS BESIDES THAT THEY WERE FEROCIOUS PREDATORS AND LIVED IN THE PLEISTOCENE. THEY BECAME EXTINCT AROUND 10,000 YEARS AGO. THEIR NAME COMES FROM THEIR LONG UPPER TEETH THAT LOOK LIKE THE BLADE OF A SABER.

QUICK, LET'S CLIMB UP THIS TREE!

I BESEECH YOU, POWERFUL GODS, USE YOUR *BLINDING FLASH* OF LIGHTNING OR THE TIGERS WILL DEVOUR US!

RIGHT! BONZO, YOU CAN USE THE FLASH TO DISORIENT THEM WHILE WE ESCAPE!

Y-Y-YES, TERSILLA... I'LL GET MY CAMERA AND...

...OOPS!

CRASH

UM...I GUESS WE'LL HAVE TO WAIT UP HERE!

GRRRR!

AT THAT VERY SAME MOMENT, IN A FOREST NOT TOO FAR AWAY...

≈NNNNG≈...IF I COULD ONLY MANAGE TO GET HOLD OF THAT AXE, I COULD USE IT TO BREAK THE BARS OF THIS CAGE!

FRUSH

FRUSH

WAIT! WE'LL HELP YOU, UNCLE GERONIMO!

???

MOLDY MOZZARELLA! BENJAMIN! BUGSY! YOU'RE SAFE!

YES, WE'RE FINE! WE'LL GET YOU OUT IN A MINUTE! BUT WHAT ARE YOU DOING HERE?

TEAK

IT WAS THE PIRATE CATS...OH, BENJAMIN, BUGSY! I'M SO HAPPY TO SEE YOU! WE WERE SO WORRIED!

BUT WHERE DID YOU DISAPPEAR TO?

RIGHT, WHERE'VE YOU BEEN? AND IN PARTICULAR, HOW DID YOU FIND US?

OH, FINDING YOU WAS EASY...WE WERE JUST LEAVING THIS FOREST WHEN WE SAW PRISONERS IN A CAGE...

AS FOR WHERE WE'VE BEEN...IT ALL HAPPENED WHEN UNCLE GERONIMO WAS ON THE BACK OF THE **MAMMOTH!**

"BENJAMIN AND I WERE RUNNING TO HELP HIM WHEN WE FELL INTO A CHASM..."

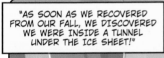
CRAAACK

"AS SOON AS WE RECOVERED FROM OUR FALL, WE DISCOVERED WE WERE INSIDE A TUNNEL UNDER THE ICE SHEET!"

"WE WALKED FOR HOURS LOOKING FOR A WAY OUT AND IN THE END WE ARRIVED NEAR HERE..."

"...IN FRONT OF A BIG WALL OF ICE, ACROSS FROM WHICH WE SAW THE FOREST!"

Y-YOU DIDN'T MEET THAT MONSTER... THE ICE GIANT?

NO, UNCLE, IT'S NOT A **MONSTER!**

IN FACT, YOU, AUNT PETUNIA, AND TRAP ABSOLUTELY MUST COME WITH US TO HELP IT.

YES, BUT...WE CAN'T RIGHT NOW: WE HAVE TO STOP THE PIRATE CATS!

UNCLE...PLEASE! IT'S REALLY **IMPORTANT!**

COME ON, GERONIMO! FOLLOW US QUICKLY!

HEY, KIDS! WHERE'RE YOU GOING? WAIT FOR US!

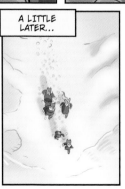
A LITTLE LATER...

THIS IS THE HOLE BUGSY AND I CAME OUT OF!

87

?!?

ROLLICKING RATS! THERE'S A BABY MAMMOTH DOWN THERE!

A BABY MAMMOTH?

WHY DIDN'T YOU SAY SO IMMEDIATELY?

WE WANTED IT TO BE A SURPRISE!

BUT WHAT IS A BABY MAMMOTH DOING HERE? HE SEEMS TO BE TRAPPED!

YES! PLUS, WE'RE RIGHT IN THAT MONSTER'S TERRITORY...THE ICE GIANT...I DON'T WANT TO RUN INTO IT!

WE NEED SHOVELS TO ENLARGE THE HOLE AND ROPE TO PULL OUT THE BABY MAMMOTH!

I HEARD THE PIRATE CATS HAVE A BLOWTORCH AND STEEL CABLES!

YOU'RE NOT THINKING OF ASKING THOSE SCOUNDRELS FOR HELP!?! AND BESIDES, WHO KNOWS WHERE THEY ARE?

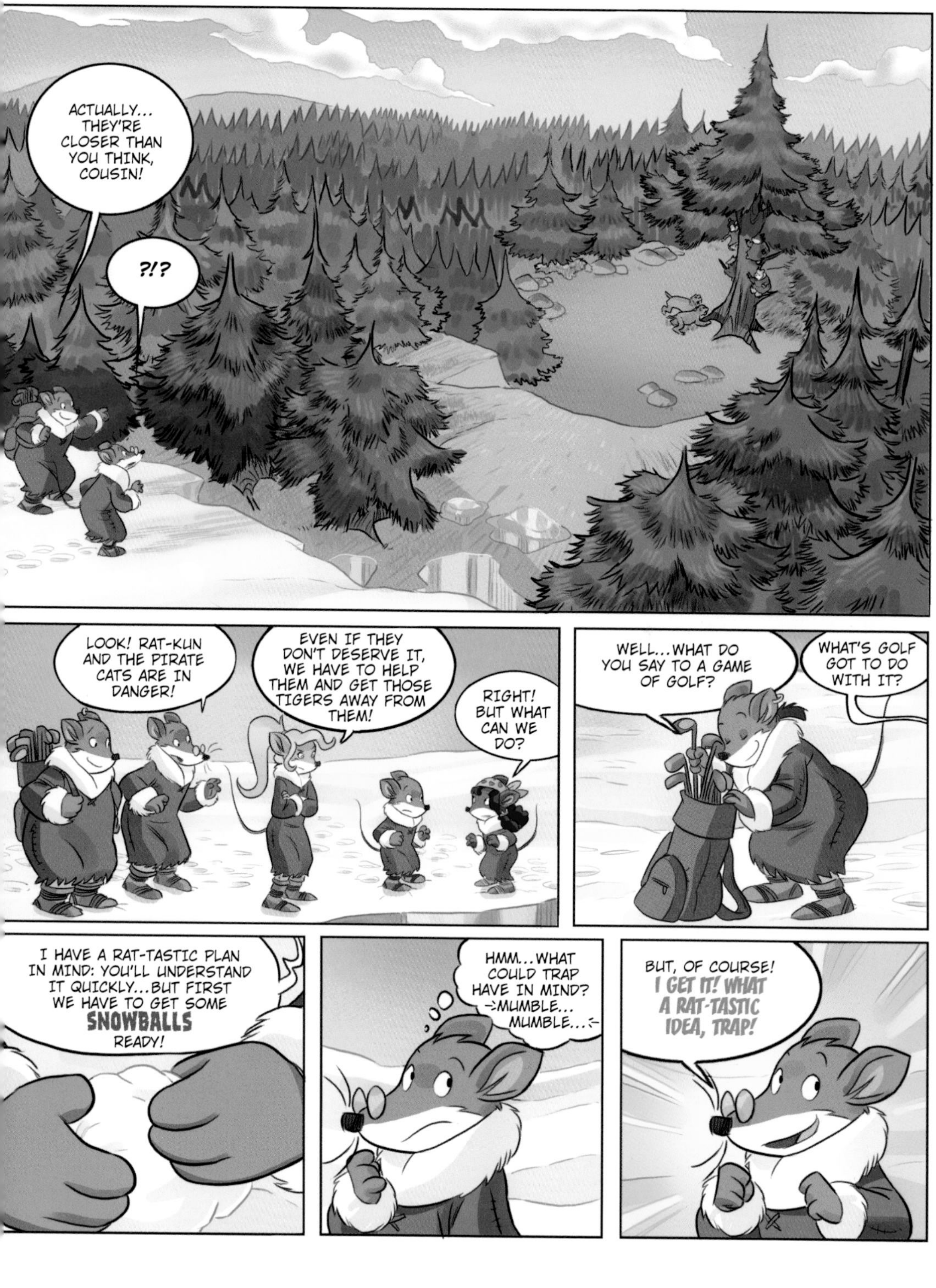
ACTUALLY... THEY'RE CLOSER THAN YOU THINK, COUSIN!
?!?
LOOK! RAT-KUN AND THE PIRATE CATS ARE IN DANGER!
EVEN IF THEY DON'T DESERVE IT, WE HAVE TO HELP THEM AND GET THOSE TIGERS AWAY FROM THEM!
RIGHT! BUT WHAT CAN WE DO?
WELL...WHAT DO YOU SAY TO A GAME OF GOLF?
WHAT'S GOLF GOT TO DO WITH IT?
I HAVE A RAT-TASTIC PLAN IN MIND: YOU'LL UNDERSTAND IT QUICKLY...BUT FIRST WE HAVE TO GET SOME SNOWBALLS READY!
HMM...WHAT COULD TRAP HAVE IN MIND? ->MUMBLE... MUMBLE...<-
BUT, OF COURSE! I GET IT! WHAT A RAT-TASTIC IDEA, TRAP!

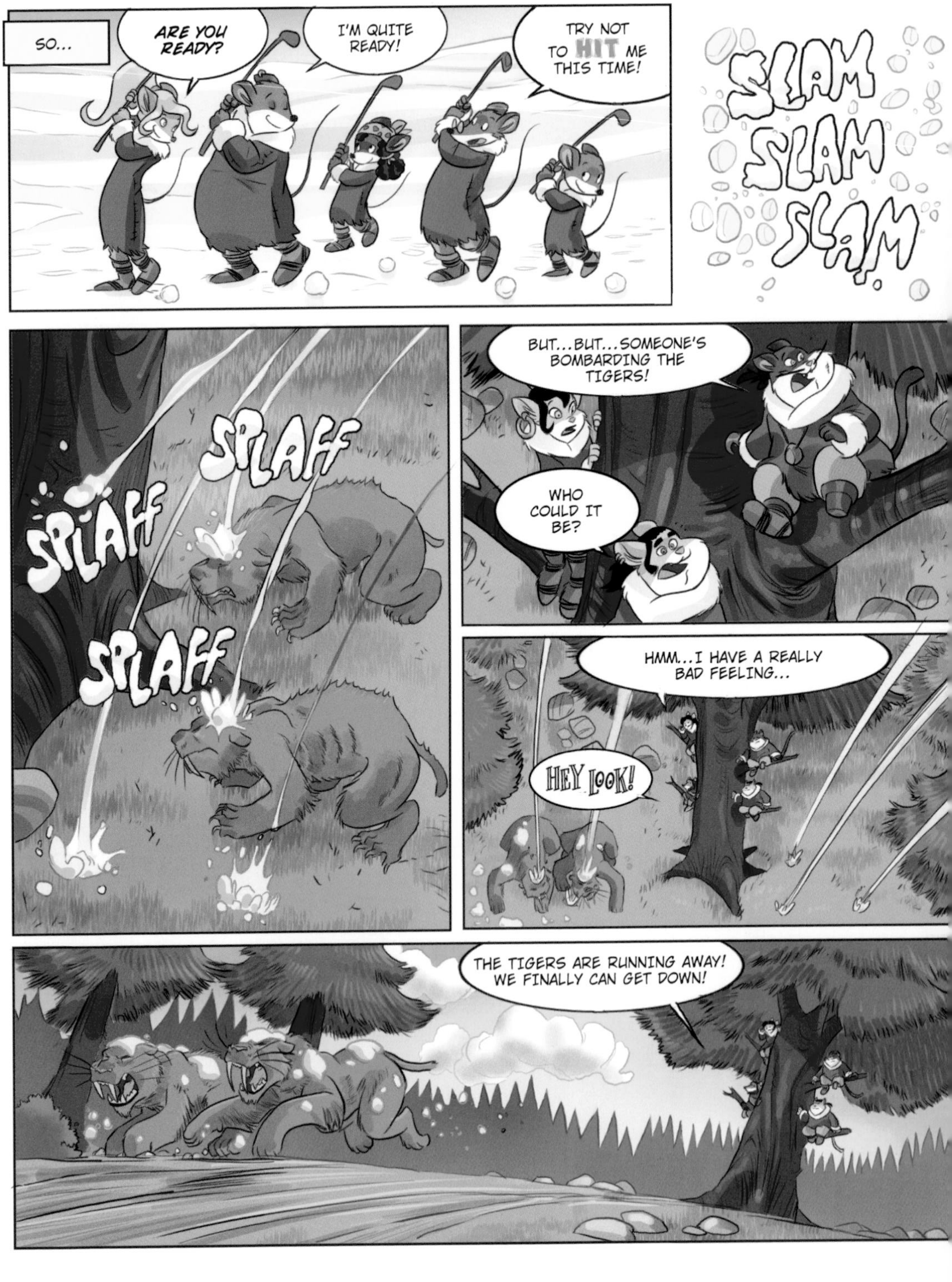
SO...
ARE YOU READY?
I'M QUITE READY!
TRY NOT TO HIT ME THIS TIME!
SLAM SLAM SLAM
SPLAFF
SPLAFF
SPLAFF
BUT...BUT...SOMEONE'S BOMBARDING THE TIGERS!
WHO COULD IT BE?
HMM...I HAVE A REALLY BAD FEELING...
HEY LOOK!
THE TIGERS ARE RUNNING AWAY! WE FINALLY CAN GET DOWN!

-SOB!- MY CAMERA'S COMPLETELY DESTROYED!

RIGHT...AND WITHOUT THAT CAMERA WE CAN'T MAKE RAT-KUN BELIEVE WE'RE GODS!

?!?

STOP RIGHT THERE, YOU CRUMMY CATS!

THE PRISONERS... MANAGED TO GET FREE!!!

YES, LUCKILY FOR YOU, RAT-KUN,... SEEING WE'RE THE ONES WHO CHASED THE TIGERS AWAY!

I...I...DON'T KNOW HOW TO THANK YOU!

OH, BELIEVE ME...THERE'LL BE A WAY!

!?

I HAVE A HUNCH WE'D BETTER ESCAPE IN A HURRY, DADDY DEAR!

BUT...THE ICE GIANT? WE'RE GOING TO LEAVE IT HERE?

SINCE WE DON'T HAVE THE CAMERA, STILTON CAN CONVINCE RAT-KUN WE AREN'T GODS AND WE'LL BE IN HOT WATER!

-GULP!-

LET'S GET OUT OF HERE!

FSHOOOM

I DON'T UNDERSTAND...WHAT HAPPENED? WHY DID THE GODS LEAVE?

I'LL EXPLAIN EVERYTHING, RAT-KUN... BUT FIRST YOU HAVE TO HELP US RESCUE A FRIEND!

I QUICKLY TOLD THE TRIBE'S LEADER ABOUT THE BABY MAMMOTH TRAPPED IN THE ICE...

~SQUEAK!~ BUT THAT'S WHERE WE SAW THE ICE GIANT!

YOU KNOW, I'M BEGINNING TO SUSPECT THAT THE ICE GIANT DOESN'T ACTUALLY EXIST...

IF IT DOESN'T EXIST... WH-WH-WHAT'S THAT?

BABARRRRRRRRRe

MOLDY MOZZARELLA!

HELP! RUN FOR IT!

?!?

I'D BETTER RACE AFTER RAT-KUN AND BRING HIM BACK!

OKAY, IN THE MEAN-TIME, I'M GOING TO TRY TO CLEAR UP THIS MYSTERY! HELP ME, TRAP!

A LITTLE LATER, WHILE I CAUGHT UP WITH RAT-KUN AND TRIED TO EXPLAIN EVERY-THING AND CALM HIM DOWN, PETUNIA AND TRAP GOT THE PIRATE CATS' BLOW-TORCH AND PUT IT TO WORK...

FZZZZ

AND WHEN WE GOT BACK, TRAP HAD ALREADY MANAGED TO MELT THE ICE AND OPEN UP A GAP...

GERONIMO, RAT-KUN, COME HERE! I'D LIKE TO PRESENT TO YOU... *THE ICE BABY!*

MENACING *MAMMOTHS!*

BUT...BUT...WHERE DID HE COME FROM? AND WHAT'S HE GOT TO DO WITH THE MONSTER?

HE JUST CAME FROM THAT ICE TUNNEL...THE MONSTER WAS HIM!

HE LOOKED LIKE A MONSTER DUE TO A STRANGE OPTICAL EFFECT OF THE ICE THAT CHANGED HIS APPEARANCE!

WHEREAS THE TRUMPETING SOUNDED SO SCARY BECAUSE IT BOOMED UNDER THE ICE SHEET!

EVERYTHING'S CLEAR NOW, BUT WHO KNOWS HOW THE BABY MAMMOTH WOUND UP OVER THERE...

HE PROBABLY GOT SEPARATED FROM HIS MOTHER AND FELL INTO A CHASM BY MISTAKE!

HEE, HEE, HEE...HE'S SO *FRIENDLY!*

AS FOR HIS MOTHER...I WONDER WHERE SHE COULD HAVE ENDED UP? MAYBE SHE'S LOOKING FOR...

SQUEEEAK! WHAT'S THAT?!?

BBAAARRR

CALAMITOUS CATS! THAT'S THE REALLY FEROCIOUS MAMMOTH I LANDED ON!

?!?

BUT OF COURSE! THAT MAMMOTH HAS TO BE HIS MAMA!

THAT'S PROBABLY WHY SHE WAS SO FURIOUS: SHE COULDN'T FIND HER BABY!

AND NOW THEY'RE FINALLY BACK TOGETHER AGAIN...->SNIFF<-... I ALWAYS FIND THESE SCENES SO TOUCHING!

YOU'RE A REGULAR ROMANTIC, COUSIN! BUT THAT'S ENOUGH BLUBBERING NOW!

PAF

THE MAMMOTHS SAID GOODBYE TO US...IN THEIR OWN WAY!

94

WELL, WE'VE COME TO THE END OF OUR ADVENTURE! ONCE AGAIN, WE'VE FOILED THE PIRATE CATS' PLANS!

YOU'VE WON AGAIN, STILTON! BUT DON'T DELUDE YOURSELF, SOONER OR LATER, WE'LL GET OUR REVENGE!

TO THANK US FOR HAVING SAVED THEM FROM THE TIGERS AND SOLVING THE MYSTERY OF THE ICE GIANT, RAT-KUN ARRANGED A BIG PARTY...

I'M GLAD YOU FOUND YOUR FRIENDS AGAIN!

SORRY WE DOUBTED YOU!

AFTER THE PARTY, WE SAID GOODBYE TO RAT-KUN, RATUK, AND RAT-RAT AND HEADED FOR THE SPEEDRAT. WE HAD TO GET BACK TO NEW MOUSE CITY!

PLEASE ACCEPT THIS NECKLACE AS A THANK YOU GIFT!

THANKS, EVERYONE!

JEWELRY

CAVE PEOPLE WORE VARIOUS TYPES OF NECKLACES AND BRACELETS. THIS JEWELRY WAS MADE OF SEA SHELLS, SMALL COLORED STONES, DRIED INSECTS, AND, ESPECIALLY, THE TEETH AND CLAWS OF WILD ANIMALS (BEARS, TIGERS, AND WOLVES), THAT HUNTERS EXHIBITED AS THEIR OWN, AUTHENTIC TROPHIES AS PROOF OF THEIR COURAGE.

ONCE AGAIN THIS TIME, PROF. VON VOLT WAS WAITING FOR US IN HIS LAB...

WELCOME BACK, MY FRIENDS! WAS YOUR TRIP A SUCCESS?

YES, PROFESSOR, EVEN THOUGH IT WAS MORE COMPLICATED AND ADVENTUROUS THAN USUAL!

WHEN WE TELL YOU WHAT THE PIRATE CAT'S GOAL WAS, YOU WON'T BELIEVE YOUR EARS!

I CAN'T WAIT TO HEAR THE WHOLE STORY...BUT FIRST, LET'S CELEBRATE!

WITH GREAT PLEASURE, PROFESS... ~SQUEEEAK!~

STOCK

OOPS...SORRY, COUSIN! YOU TOLD ME WHEN THE MISSION WAS OVER I COULD START TRAINING AGAIN!

MY POOR HEAD! THAT HURTS!

HA, HA, HA!

MY DEAR RODENT FRIENDS, FAREWELL UNTIL THE NEXT ADVENTURE... ANOTHER WHISKERFUL OF AN ADVENTURE, WRITTEN BY STILTON...GERONIMO STILTON!

WHO STOLE THE MONA LISA?

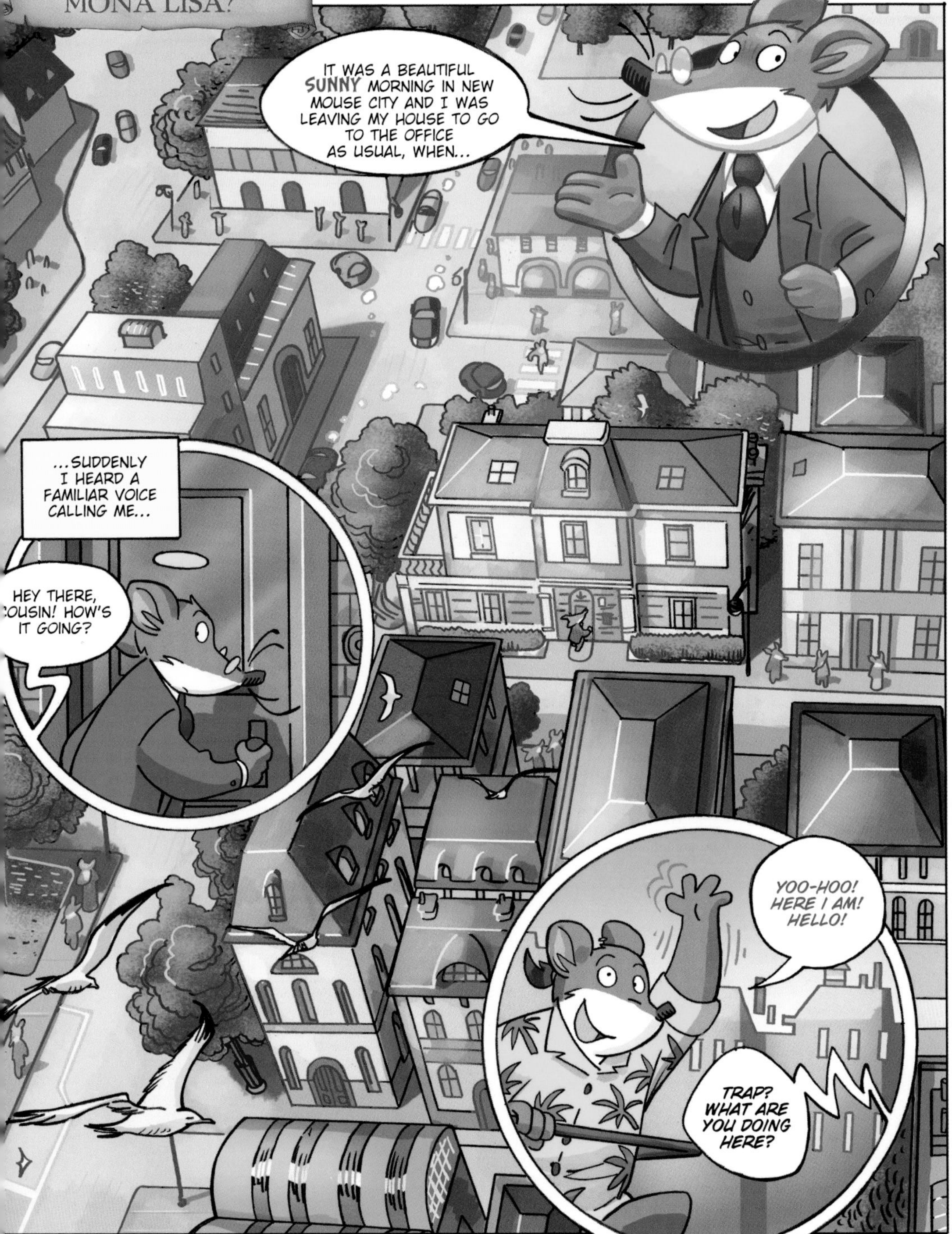
IT WAS A BEAUTIFUL SUNNY MORNING IN NEW MOUSE CITY AND I WAS LEAVING MY HOUSE TO GO TO THE OFFICE AS USUAL, WHEN...
...SUDDENLY I HEARD A FAMILIAR VOICE CALLING ME...
HEY THERE, COUSIN! HOW'S IT GOING?
YOO-HOO! HERE I AM! HELLO!
TRAP? WHAT ARE YOU DOING HERE?

HOP ON BOARD! I'LL TAKE YOU TO YOUR OFFICE IN MY RICKSHAW!

YOUR RICKSHAW?!? UMM...OKAY!

OH, SORRY! I FORGOT TO INTRODUCE MYSELF... MY NAME IS STILTON, *Geronimo Stilton!* AND I EDIT THE *RODENT'S GAZETTE.*

GO SLOWLY! YOU KNOW I GET CARSICK!

THEN **YOU** DRIVE. THAT WAY YOU WON'T WORRY!

WHAT?!? ME? BUT... BUT...WHY?

COME ON, GERONIMO, DON'T BE ALL SAD AND WHINY! IF YOU DRIVE, YOU'LL FEEL JUST FINE!

BUT... BUT... I DON'T KNOW IF I CAN DO IT!

I GRANT YOU THE HONOR AND AWE OF DRIVING MY BRAND NEW RICKSHAW... THE ONLY ONE I HAVE!

COME ON, WE'RE WASTING TIME. LET'S GO!

A LITTLE LATER, ON THE STREETS OF NEW MOUSE CITY...

YOU'RE A VERY GOOD DRIVER, COUSIN!

OH, COULD YOU STOP AT THE BAKERY AND LEND ME SOME DOUGH FOR SOME CAKE?

~SIGH!~

MEANWHILE IN CATBURG, THE CAPITAL OF CAT ISLAND...

ANY **NEWS**, TERSILLA?

NONE YET, DADDY DEAR!

THE EXPERTS CONFIRM THAT THIS PARCHMENT FOUND IN THE GALLEON DATES BACK TO 1500...

...BUT IT'S WRITTEN IN A MYSTERIOUS CODE THEY CAN'T DECIPHER!

IT MUST HAVE DIRECTIONS FOR FINDING A CAT-TASTIC TREASURE!

WE'LL PROCEED WITH OUR PLAN! GET READY TO LEAVE FOR MOUSE ISLAND!

MOUSE ISLAND?! WHAT'RE WE GOING TO DO THERE?

SILENCE, YOU PAIN IN THE TAIL*!

MEOOOW!

*PAIN IN THE NECK

MEOW DOWN,* BONZO! CATARDONE WILL EXPLAIN EVERYTHING TO YOU ALONG THE WAY!

FOR NOW, WE'VE FIGURED OUT THAT SOMETHING'S WRITTEN ON THE PARCHMENT AND WE'RE GOING TO TEACH GERONIMO STILTON A LOVELY LESSON...HEE, HEE, HEE!

*CALM DOWN

THAT NIGHT, IN NEW MOUSE CITY...

RONF RONF

RONF RONF

Rrinnggg... rinnggg...

...rrinnggg... attention, call for Geronimo Stilton... rrinngg...

...rrinnggg... Geronimo, it's Ampy Von Volt. Do you hear me?

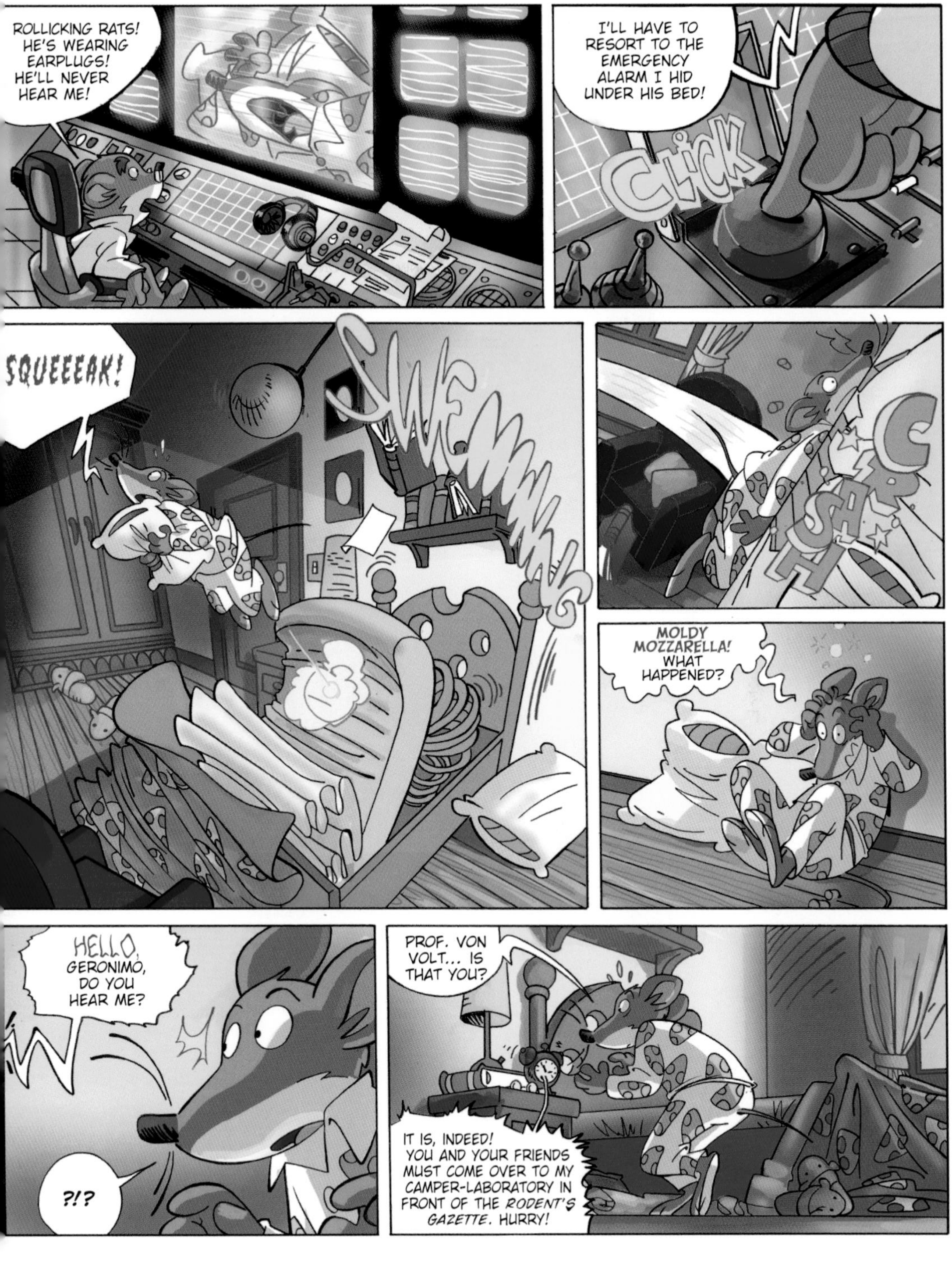
ROLLICKING RATS! HE'S WEARING EARPLUGS! HE'LL NEVER HEAR ME!
I'LL HAVE TO RESORT TO THE EMERGENCY ALARM I HID UNDER HIS BED!
CLICK
SQUEEEAK!
SWEEEMMMMMNG
CRASH
MOLDY MOZZARELLA! WHAT HAPPENED?
HELLO, GERONIMO, DO YOU HEAR ME?
?!?
PROF. VON VOLT... IS THAT YOU?
IT IS, INDEED! YOU AND YOUR FRIENDS MUST COME OVER TO MY CAMPER-LABORATORY IN FRONT OF THE RODENT'S GAZETTE. HURRY!

HISTORY IS IN DANGER AGAIN!

→GULP!← I'LL GET DRESSED AND BE RIGHT THERE, PROFESSOR!

I MUST LET THE OTHERS KNOW. I HOPE I CAN FIND A TAXI RIGHT AWAY!

HEY THERE, COUSIN. NEED A LIFT?

OH, NO!

LATER, ALONG WITH THEA, TRAP, BENJAMIN, AND BUGSY WUGSY, I ARRIVED AT VON VOLT'S LAB...

HERE WE ARE, PROFESSOR... →PANT, PANT←...

?!?

GERONIMO, IS EVERYTHING ALL RIGHT?

Y- YES...

SORRY TO BOTHER YOU, BUT IT'S AN EMERGENCY!

IS IT THE PIRATE CATS AGAIN, PROFESSOR?

UNFORTUNATELY, YES, BUGSY: THEY'RE TRAVELING INTO THE PAST AGAIN WITH THEIR TIME MACHINE!

THOSE CRUMMY CATS WANT TO CHANGE HISTORY TO THEIR BENEFIT!

ARE YOU OKAY, THEA? YOU'RE AS WHITE AS A SLICE OF MOZZARELLA!

M-ME? YES... YES!

IT'S JUST... CAN'T SEEM TO DIGEST THE TALEGGIO CHEESE FONDUE I HAD FOR DINNER.

WHERE ARE THE PIRATE CATS HEADED THIS TIME?

TO AMBOISE, IN FRANCE, IN THE YEAR 1517!

FRANCE

OWES ITS NAME TO THE ANCIENT GERMANIC POPULATION, THE FRANKS, WHO CONQUERED THE REGION IN THE FOURTH CENTURY AD. THEIR FIRST KING, CLOVIS (481-511), CAME FROM THE MEROVINGIAN LINE. AFTER THE FRENCH REVOLUTION, IN 1789, FRANCE WAS PROCLAIMED A REPUBLIC, BUT UNDER NAPOLEON BONAPARTE, IT BECAME AN EMPIRE (1804). AFTER VARIOUS EVENTS, FRANCE WAS ONCE AGAIN PROCLAIMED A REPUBLIC IN 1871, WITH PARIS AS ITS CAPITAL.

B-B-BUT... HOW DO YOU KNOW THIS?

?!?

POOR THEA, SHE REALLY MUST HAVE EATEN TOO MUCH!

I'M SURPRISED BY YOUR QUESTION, THEA! BY NOW YOU SHOULD KNOW ABOUT THE TEMPOGRAPH, THE DEVICE I USE TO MONITOR THE COURSE OF HISTORY!

UM... RIGHT, OF COURSE... THE TEMPOGRAPH... HOW SILLY OF ME!

THAT'S NOT IT! THAT'S JUST AN OLD CUCKOO CLOCK!

KOO-KOO

?!?

THIS IS THE TEMPOGRAPH!

YOU MUST HAVE EATEN SOMETHING REALLY GREASY, LITTLE COUSIN!

GETTING BACK TO THE PIRATE CATS, I'M AFRAID THEIR TARGET MAY BE THE FAMOUS SCIENTIST AND ARTIST **LEONARDO DA VINCI.** AT THAT TIME HE LIVED IN THE FRENCH TOWN OF AMBOISE, IN THE CASTLE OF CLOUX, AS A GUEST OF FRANCIS I, THE KING OF FRANCE!

LEONARDO DA VINCI (1452-1519) PAINTER, SCULPTOR, ARCHITECT, SCIENTIST, AND INVENTOR LEONARDO DA VINCI IS CONSIDERED ONE OF THE GREATEST GENIUSES WHO EVER LIVED. HE WAS BORN IN VINCI, A VILLAGE NEAR FLORENCE, IN ITALY. HIS MOST FAMOUS WORKS OF ART INCLUDE "THE LAST SUPPER" WHICH HE PAINTED IN THE CHURCH OF SANTA MARIA DELLA GRAZIE IN MILAN AND THE PAINTING, "LA GIOCONDA," ALSO KNOWN AS THE "MONA LISA," WHICH IS KEPT TODAY AT THE LOUVRE MUSEUM IN PARIS.

UMM... –GULP– ARE YOU SAYING...?

THAT THEY WANT TO STEAL A *PAINTBRUSH AND PAINTS?*

MAYBE THEY WANT TO STEAL THE MONA LISA!

THE ONLY WAY TO FIND OUT IS FOR US TO GO THE SIXTEENTH CENTURY, TO AMBOISE, TOO.

A LITTLE LATER, WE WERE IN THE SPEEDRAT, READY TO GO...

ONBOARD ARE CLOTHES FROM THE PERIOD AND EARPLUGS THAT WILL LET YOU SPEAK THE LOCAL LANGUAGE!

THANKS, PROFESSOR! DON'T WORRY, WE'LL STOP THE PIRATE CATS!

DO YOU FEEL LIKE DRIVING, THEA?

OF COURSE, I FEEL LIKE IT! WHAT A QUESTION!

LET'S SEE... HOW DO I TURN THIS THING ON?

HMMM... LET'S TRY THIS BUTTON!

CLICK

?!?

SWOOOM

SRASH

HMPH...

THAT'S THE BUTTON FOR THE EJECTION SEATS!

MAYBE YOU SHOULD DRIVE, TRAP!

MEANWHILE, THE PIRATE CATS HAD LANDED NEAR AMBOISE IN THE YEAR 1517 IN THE MIDDLE OF THE RENAISSANCE...

THERE WE GO, THE CATJET IS COMPLETELY **CAMOUFLAGED!**

DID YOU REMEMBER TO BRING THE **PAINT** CANS?

THE RENAISSANCE
THE PERIOD IN HISTORY FROM THE END OF THE 1300S AND THE MIDDLE OF THE 1500S IS CALLED THE RENAISSANCE. THE NAME COMES FROM THE FACT THAT AFTER THE MIDDLE AGES, WHICH WERE CHARACTERIZED BY POVERTY AND LITTLE ECONOMIC GROWTH, EUROPE EXPERIENCED A PERIOD OF QUICK DEVELOPMENT, ACTUALLY A "REBIRTH," BOTH ECONOMICALLY, ARTISTICALLY, AND CULTURALLY. "RENAISSANCE" MEANS "REBIRTH" IN FRENCH.

YES, YES... EVEN THOUGH I'M NOT SURE WHAT WE'RE USING THEM FOR!

I'LL TELL YOU LATER! IS THE REST OF THE PLAN CLEAR?

HMM... SURE! WE HAVE TO KIDNAP LEONARDO DA VINCI AND BRING HIM WITH US TO CATBURG!

EXACTLY! ACCORDING TO TERSILLA, HE'S THE ONLY ONE WHO CAN DECODE THE MYSTERIOUS PARCHMENT!

106

LEONARDO WILL BE ABLE TO TRANSLATE THE CODE. THEN WE CAN ALSO ASK HIM TO INVENT A RAT-CATCHING MACHINE!

BUT HOW ARE WE GOING TO KIDNAP HIM?

WE'LL PRETEND TO BE TWO FRENCH **PAINTERS** WHO WANT TO BECOME HIS PUPILS!

PAINTING IN THE RENAISSANCE

DURING THIS PERIOD, PAINTERS PERFECTED THE USE OF PERSPECTIVE TO PORTRAY THE DEPTH AND PROPORTIONS OF OBJECTS JUST AS WE SEE THEM (FOR EXAMPLE, BY DRAWING OBJECTS THAT ARE FAR AWAY SMALLER). PAINTERS ALSO PAID A GREAT DEAL OF ATTENTION TO STUDYING THE BODY AND ITS MOVEMENT ANATOMICALLY.

AND WHEN WILL TERSILLA GET HERE?

SHE'LL CATCH UP WITH US AT THE RIGHT TIME! HER JOB IS VITAL FOR OUR **PLAN** TO SUCCEED!

COME ON! LET'S PUT ON OUR MOUSE MASKS AND CLOTHING FROM THE PERIOD.

AFTER A FEW MINUTES...

LEONARDO WILL NEVER SUSPECT WE'RE CATS!

NOW WE'RE JUST MISSING THE FINAL TOUCH!

UMM... AND THAT WOULD BE?

PAINTERS ALWAYS HAVE PAINT ALL OVER THEM!

SPLAFF

MEOW!

NOW YOU REALLY LOOK LIKE A PAINTER! SHALL I GIVE YOU A COAT OF YELLOW PAINT, TOO?

FIRST LET ME GIVE YOU A HAND!

-;GULP!;-

HOW *DARE YOU!?* GRRR... I'LL... I'LL... *ATOMIZE** YOU!

*DESTROY YO

A LITTLE LATER, THE CATS ARRIVED AT THE CASTLE OF CLOUX.

THE CASTLE OF CLOUX WAS LOCATED ONLY 500 METERS FROM THE ROYAL CASTLE OF AMBOISE. AT THE REQUEST OF KING FRANCIS I OF FRANCE, LEONARDO DA VINCI STAYED THERE FROM 1517-1519, THE YEAR HE DIED. TODAY THE CASTLE IS CALLED CLOS LUCE AND HOUSES A MUSEUM DEDICATED TO THE GREAT ARTIST.

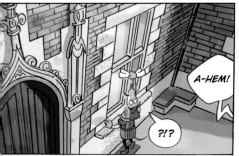

A-HEM!

?!?

MELTING CAMEMBERT!

GOOD DAY! IS THIS THE HOME OF MASTER LEONARDO?

WH-WH-WHO ARE YOU? WH-WH-WHAT DO YOU WANT?

MY NAME IS CATARD OF CAT AND THIS IS BONZETON LEBONZE. WE'RE PAINTERS!

PAINTERS?!

SURE, DON'T YOU SEE HOW WE'RE COVERED WITH PAINT?

FORGIVE ME, I THOUGHT YOU WERE VAGRANTS! I'M BATTISTA, MASTER LEONARDO'S SERVANT!

WELL, BATTISTA, COULD YOU TELL THE MASTER THAT WE'D LIKE TO MEET HIM?

I'M SORRY, BUT HE'S BUSY WITH AN EXPERIMENT AND CANNOT BE DISTURBED!

LEONARDO'S MACHINES

BESIDES BEING A GREAT ARTIST, LEONARDO WAS ALSO A CLEVER INVENTOR AND SCIENTIST. HE DEVISED MACHINES THAT CAN BE CONSIDERED THE "ANCESTORS" OF MANY MODERN INVENTIONS, SUCH AS CARS, BICYCLES, MOTORBOATS, AND EVEN A HELICOPTER. HE WAS THE FIRST TO ENVISION DEVICES THAT HUMANS WOULD ONE DAY USE TO FLY WITH.

NOW WHAT'RE WE GOING TO DO?

HMPH... WILL HE BE BUSY FOR A WHILE?

IT DEPENDS ON WHETHER HE IS ABLE TO STOP!

TO STOP?!

GET OUT OF THE WAY, OVER THERE! MAKE WAY! MAKE WAY!

UH?

OUT OF THE WAY! I'VE LOST CONTROL OF THE MACHINE!

WROOOOMM

RUN FOR YOUR LIFE!

HELPPPPP!

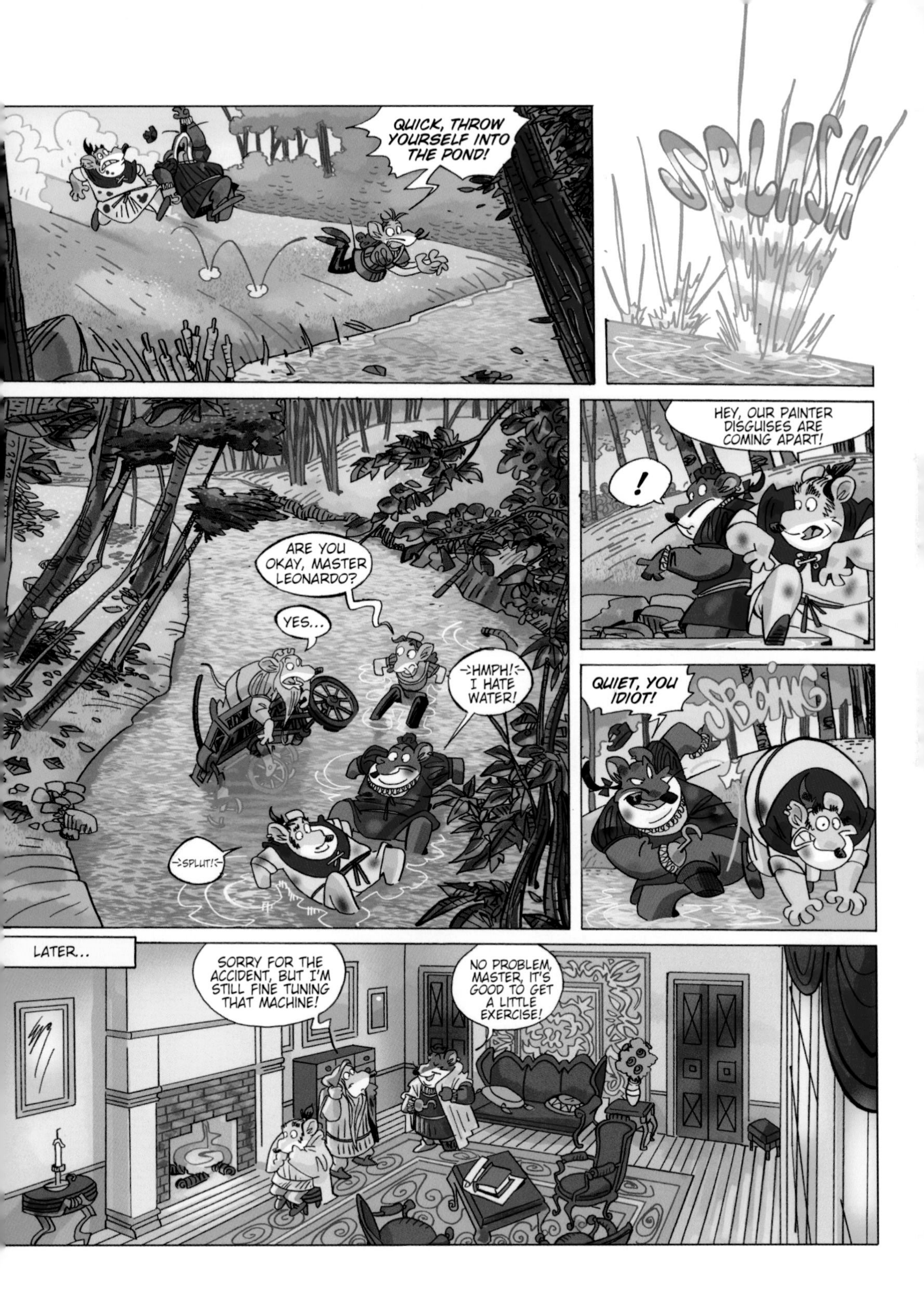
QUICK, THROW YOURSELF INTO THE POND!
SPLASH
ARE YOU OKAY, MASTER LEONARDO?
YES...
HMPH! I HATE WATER!
SPLUT!
HEY, OUR PAINTER DISGUISES ARE COMING APART!
!
QUIET, YOU IDIOT!
SBOING
LATER...
SORRY FOR THE ACCIDENT, BUT I'M STILL FINE TUNING THAT MACHINE!
NO PROBLEM, MASTER, IT'S GOOD TO GET A LITTLE EXERCISE!

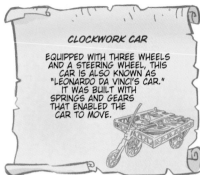

CLOCKWORK CAR

EQUIPPED WITH THREE WHEELS AND A STEERING WHEEL, THIS CAR IS ALSO KNOWN AS "LEONARDO DA VINCI'S CAR." IT WAS BUILT WITH SPRINGS AND GEARS THAT ENABLED THE CAR TO MOVE.

BATTISTA MENTIONED TO ME THAT YOU'RE ALSO **PAINTERS!**

ACTUALLY WE'RE JUST HUMBLE BEGINNERS!

WE WANT YOU TO TEACH US ALL THE SECRETS OF PAINTING!

I'M SORRY TO DISAPPOINT YOU, BUT I SELDOM DO ANY PAINTING NOWADAYS!

I DO NEED ASSISTANTS, HOWEVER, TO TEST-DRIVE MY MACHINES!

UH-OH!

UM... ⇒GULP!⇐... WE'D BE HONORED!

BUT I WARN YOU: IT'S VERY DANGEROUS WORK!

WE CA... ⇒AHEM⇐ RODENTS ARE AFRAID OF NOTHING!

THEN YOU CAN HELP ME WITH MY EXPERIMENTS AND I'LL GIVE YOU PAINTING LESSONS IN EXCHANGE!

IT'S A DEAL!

HMM... I PREDICT A *SEA* OF TROUBLES!

IN THE MEANTIME, MY FRIENDS AND I HAD ARRIVED NEAR AMBOISE.

NICE LANDING, TRAP!

THANKS, COUSIN! YOU'RE TOO KIND!

ACTUALLY... I WAS BEING SARCASTIC!

HEY, WE'RE SAFE AND SOUND, RIGHT?

YES, BUT WE'RE UP A TREE!

SO? WE WON'T EVEN HAVE TO HIDE THE SPEEDRAT!

BUT I'M AFRAID OF HEIGHTS! HOW AM I SUPPOSED TO GET DOWN?

YOU DON'T WANT ME TO CARRY YOU DOWN ON MY BACK, DO YOU, COUSIN?

WHILE YOU KEEP TALKING, I'M *LEAVING...*

?!?

113

WOW! WHAT A **RAT-TASTIC** LEAP!

-GULP!-

A FEW MINUTES LATER, AFTER STARTING TO GET READY...

DON'T FORGET TO PUT ON PROFESSOR VON VOLT'S EARPHONES!

ARE WE GOING STRAIGHT TO THE CASTLE OF CLOUX, UNCLE GERONIMO?

YES, LEONARDO IS OUR ONLY **CLUE!**

SO LET'S GET GOING!

HOW EXCITING: WE'RE IN THE MIDDLE OF THE RENAISSANCE!

AND SOON WE'LL EVEN MEET LEONARDO DA VINCI!

THIS IS THE CASTLE OF AMBOISE! CLOUX IS A LITTLE FARTHER ON!

AMBOISE CASTLE

WAS BUILT IN THE 13TH CENTURY ON A BLUFF OVERLOOKING THE LOIRE RIVER IN CENTRAL FRANCE. IN THE FOLLOWING CENTURIES, LARGE GARDENS AND WIDE TERRACES WERE CREATED HANGING OVER THE RIVER. KING FRANCIS I OF FRANCE USED AMBOISE CASTLE AS HIS HOME WHEN HE STAYED IN THE LOIRE VALLEY.

SOON, WE REACHED THE CASTLE OF CLOUX...

STRANGE, NO ONE SEEMS TO BE **AROUND**...

I'LL TRY KNOCKING ON THE DOOR!

BUT... WE CAN'T DISTURB LEONARDO WITHOUT A REASON!

GERONIMO, YOU TOLD US LEONARDO WAS OUR ONLY CLUE!

WINGS

AMONG HIS DIFFERENT INVENTIONS, LEONARDO DESIGNED WINGS FOR FLYING THAT WERE LIKE THE WINGS OF A BAT AND COULD BE ATTACHED TO A FLYING MACHINE. THE WINGS WERE MADE OF FABRIC STRETCHED OVER A WOOD AND BAMBOO FRAME.

AND THIS IS MY NEPHEW BELMOUSE, HIS FRIEND BUGSETTE, MY SISTER THEA AND MY COUSIN TRAPO FALON.

WE ARE MERCHANTS FROM MARSEILLE... AND WOULD LIKE TO BUY ONE OF YOUR WORKS OF ART!

MARSEILLE? MERCHANTS???

WELCOME! BATTISTA WILL GET A ROOM READY FOR YOU IMMEDIATELY!

YOU'RE VERY KIND!

GOOD DAY, MASTER LEONARDO, I SEE YOU HAVE MANY VISITORS TODAY!

WHAT?

AH, GOOD DAY, YOUR MAJESTY!

THAT MUST BE KING FRANCIS I OF FRANCE!

THEN WE HAVE TO BOW, BUGSY!

FRANCIS I (1494-1547)

WAS BORN IN COGNAC, FRANCE IN 1494. IN 1514 HE WAS GRANTED THE TITLE OF DUKE OF VALOIS AND MARRIED CLAUDIA, DAUGHTER OF KING LOUIS XII OF FRANCE, BECOMING HIS LEGITIMATE SUCCESSOR. ONCE HE ASCENDED TO THE THRONE, FRANCIS I FOCUSED PRIMARILY ON FOREIGN POLICY, BUT HE NEVER LET THAT END HIS PASSION FOR THE ARTS AND LITERATURE. MANY ITALIAN POETS AND ARTISTS BESIDES LEONARDO LIVED AT THE COURT OF THE KING.

ARE THESE RODENTS YOUR NEW ASSISTANTS?

ONLY CATARD AND BONZETON... THE OTHERS ARE MERCHANTS WHO WANT TO BUY MY PAINTINGS!

WHAT? YOU'RE NOT THINKING OF SELLING THE PAINTINGS YOU PROMISED TO ME, RIGHT?

I WOULD NEVER DARE OFFEND MY PATRON LIKE THAT!

I SHOULD CERTAINLY HOPE NOT!

YOU KNOW THEY'RE PREPARED TO PAY ANY PRICE JUST TO HAVE THE PAINTING OF THE **SMILING LADY!**

HUH?

I CAME SPECIFICALLY TO ADMIRE IT!

I WOULD BE HAPPY TO ACCOMPANY YOU TO MY STUDIO, SIRE! AND WITH YOUR PERMISSION, I WOULD ALSO LIKE TO SHOW THE PAINTING TO MY NEW FRIENDS!

SO BE IT! BUT DON'T FORGET THAT YOU PROMISED IT TO ME!

LA GIOCONDA

LA GIOCONDA, ALSO CALLED THE "MONA LISA," IS LEONARDO DA VINCI'S MOST FAMOUS PAINTING. HE PAINTED IT BETWEEN 1503 AND 1506 ON A PLANK OF POPLAR WOOD, USING OIL PAINTS. WE STILL AREN'T CERTAIN ABOUT THE IDENTITY OF THE WOMAN HE PAINTED. ACCORDING TO SOME SCHOLARS, SHE WAS MONA LISA GHERARDINI, THE WIFE OF FRANCESCO BARTOLOMEO DEL GIOCONDO (WHOSE NAME WAS USED FOR THE PAINTING). THE PAINTING WAS MADE IN FLORENCE AND AFTERWARDS LEONARDO TOOK IT WITH HIM WHEREVER HE LIVED.

YOU'VE SURPASSED YOURSELF WITH THIS PAINTING!

YOU FLATTER ME, MAJESTY! I'M GLAD IT PLEASES YOU!

I'M STAYING HERE TO CONTEMPLATE THE PAINTING! YOU GO ON AHEAD!

YES, MASTER LEONARDO, LET US SEE ALL YOUR WORKS OF ART... WE'RE HERE JUST FOR THAT REASON!

TO TELL YOU THE TRUTH, I PROMISED MY ASSISTANTS...

DON'T WORRY ABOUT US, **MASTER**, YOUR GUESTS ARE MORE IMPORTANT!

ESPECIALLY AFTER THE THRILL OF FLYING...WE DESERVE A NICE CATNAP!

OH, JUST SO YOU KNOW, I'LL LEAVE THROUGH THE TUNNEL THAT CONNECTS OUR TWO CASTLES!

THE UNDERGROUND TUNNEL

FRANCIS I ADMIRED LEONARDO'S GENIUS SO MUCH THAT HE BUILT AN UNDERGROUND TUNNEL BETWEEN THE CASTLE OF AMBOISE, HIS RESIDENCE, AND THE CASTLE OF CLOUX, WHERE LEONARDO LIVED. THAT WAY, HE COULD GET TO LEONARDO'S STUDIO AT ANY HOUR OF THE DAY OR NIGHT TO ADMIRE HIS WORK.

LATER, AFTER SHOWING US ALL HIS WORK, LEONARDO WENT BACK TO HIS EXPERIMENTS...

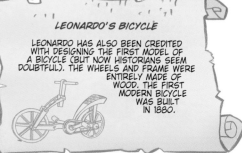

LEONARDO'S BICYCLE

LEONARDO HAS ALSO BEEN CREDITED WITH DESIGNING THE FIRST MODEL OF A BICYCLE (BUT NOW HISTORIANS SEEM DOUBTFUL). THE WHEELS AND FRAME WERE ENTIRELY MADE OF WOOD. THE FIRST MODERN BICYCLE WAS BUILT IN 1880.

...WHILE WE GOT TOGETHER IN THE ROOM THEY'D GIVEN TRAP AND ME.

SO... DID YOU NOTICE ANYTHING SUSPICIOUS?

YES, SOMETHING IS STRANGE ABOUT HIS TWO ASSISTANTS.

IN FACT, THEY'RE A LITTLE WEIRD!

BUT THAT'S NOT PROOF THEY'RE CATS.

WHAT IF LEONARDO ISN'T THE CAT'S REAL TARGET?

RIGHT... MAYBE THEY'RE MORE INTERESTED IN THE KING!

TRAP'S NOT ALTOGETHER WRONG! MAYBE FRANCIS I COULD BE THEIR TARGET!

MAYBE THEY WANT TO KICK HIM OFF THE FRENCH THRONE.

RIGHT, BUT...WHY DIDN'T THEY GO STRAIGHT TO PARIS?

WE DON'T KNOW... FOR NOW, IT'S BETTER IF WE STAY AT CLOUX AND KEEP AN EYE ON LEONARDO'S ASSISTANTS AND SERVANT!

RAT-TASTIC! WE'LL SEE LEONARDO IN ACTION WITH HIS MACHINES!

IF THEY ALL WORK LIKE THE WINGS DID, IT'LL BE LOTS OF LAUGHS!

AT MIDNIGHT...

122

CREEK

-SNORE...
SNORE...

CIAO, TERSILLA! YOU'VE FINALLY ARRIVED...

I WAS STARTING TO WORRY... BONZO KEEPS MOUSING UP!*

DON'T WORRY, DADDY DEAR! IS EVERY-THING GOING AS PLANNED WITH LEONARDO?

*MESSING UP

OF COURSE! BONZO AND I ARE TESTING A KIND OF MOTORBOAT WITH HIM TOMORROW!

PERFECT! I'LL TAKE ADVANTAGE OF THAT TO BEGIN THE SECOND PART OF OUR PLAN!

I'D BETTER GO NOW! I ALREADY RAN QUITE A RISK COMING TO YOU!

SHOULD I TELL BONZO ANYTHING WHEN HE WAKES UP?

JUST TO STOP MOUSING UP!

THE NEXT MORNING, LEONARDO SUMMONED US TO THE BANKS OF THE CHANNEL TO WATCH HIM LAUNCH HIS "PADDLE BOAT."

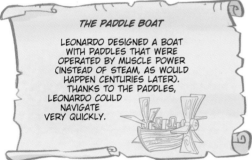

THE PADDLE BOAT

LEONARDO DESIGNED A BOAT WITH PADDLES THAT WERE OPERATED BY MUSCLE POWER (INSTEAD OF STEAM, AS WOULD HAPPEN CENTURIES LATER). THANKS TO THE PADDLES, LEONARDO COULD NAVIGATE VERY QUICKLY.

WHEN I SHOW YOU HOW THIS BOAT WORKS, YOU'LL BE SPEECHLESS!

UMM... MASTER LEONARDO... I HAVE TO TELL YOU SOMETHING...

LATER, BONZETON! I'M TALKING!

MASTER LEONARDO, IT'S IMPORTANT!

HMPH! TELL ME WHAT YOU WANT?

THE BOAT IS SINKING!

FRANTIC FRESH FRESCOES!

HURRY! START PADDLING!

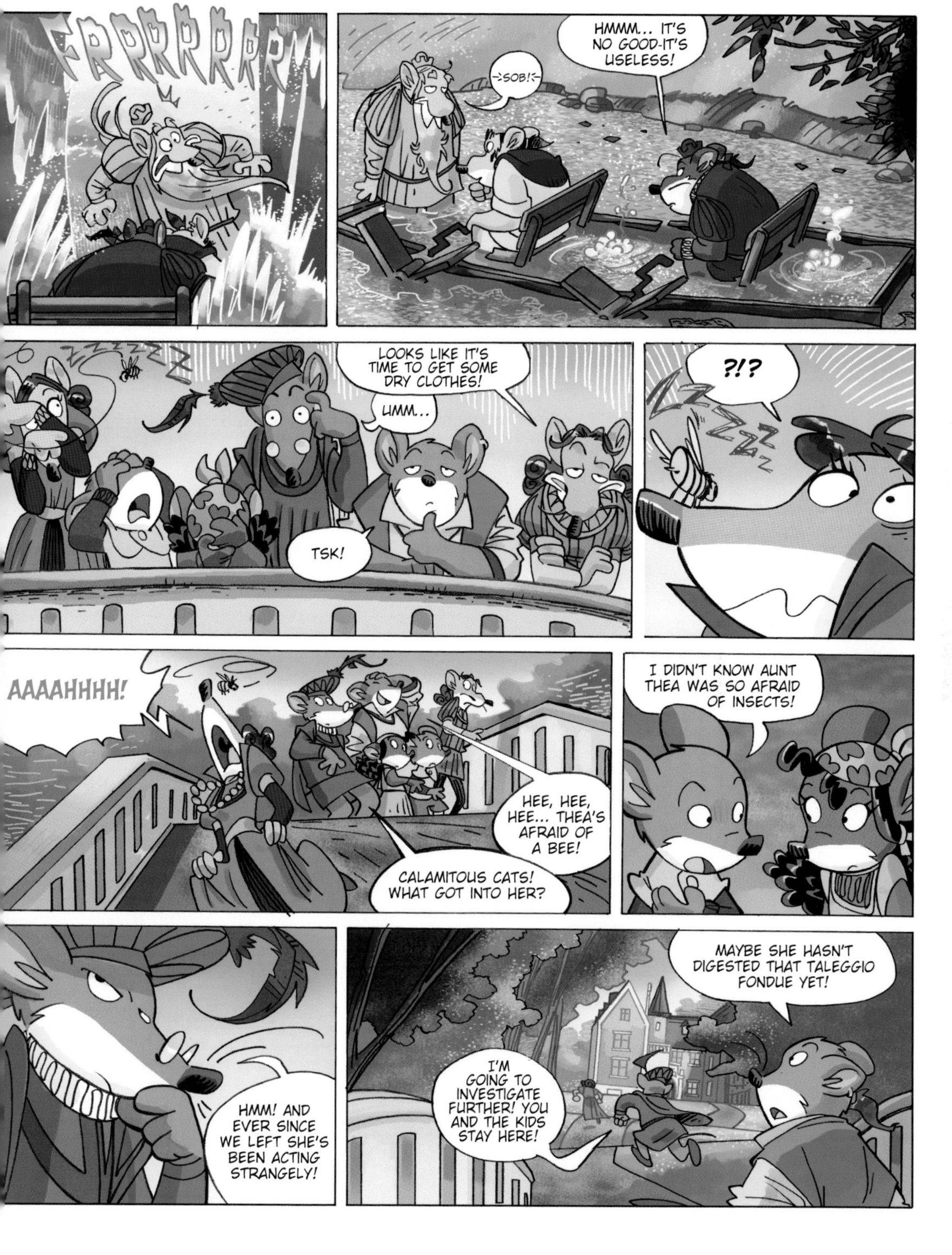
FRRRRRRRRM
-SOB!-
HMMM... IT'S NO GOOD-IT'S USELESS!
LOOKS LIKE IT'S TIME TO GET SOME DRY CLOTHES!
UMM...
TSK!
?!?
AAAAHHHH!
HEE, HEE, HEE... THEA'S AFRAID OF A BEE!
CALAMITOUS CATS! WHAT GOT INTO HER?
I DIDN'T KNOW AUNT THEA WAS SO AFRAID OF INSECTS!
HMM! AND EVER SINCE WE LEFT SHE'S BEEN ACTING STRANGELY!
MAYBE SHE HASN'T DIGESTED THAT TALEGGIO FONDUE YET!
I'M GOING TO INVESTIGATE FURTHER! YOU AND THE KIDS STAY HERE!

A LITTLE LATER, AT THE CASTLE OF CLOUX...

WHO KNOWS WHERE THEA IS...? SHE'S NOT IN HER ROOM...

THE DOOR TO LEONARDO'S STUDIO IS OPEN! IS SHE HERE?

MOLDY MOZZARELLA!

YOUR MAJESTY, ARE YOU OKAY?

OOOOHHH... WH-WH-WHERE AM I? WHAT HAPPENED TO ME?

CRUMBLING CAMEMBERT! NOW I REMEMBER!

I HEARD A RUSTLING BEHIND ME AND THEN... SOMEONE HIT ME ON THE **HEAD!**

THERE'S A CANDELABRA ON THE FLOOR! IT COULD HAVE BEEN USED TO HIT YOU!

126

HIT ME? THE KING OF FRANCE? WHAT AN OUTRAGE! GUARDS! **GUARDSSSSSSSSS!**

WHAT A HUGE VOICE! HE'S LIKE GRANDPA TANK!

YIKES! I NEARLY FELL! BUT... BUT... WHAT'S THIS?

A PINK NECKLACE? WHERE DID I JUST SEE IT...?

OH, NO! NOW I REMEMBER WHERE I SAW IT...

MAJESTY... WHAT HAPPENED? WAS THAT YOU *SCREAMING?*

A STRANGER GOT INTO THE STUDIO AND HIT ME ON THE HEAD WITH A CANDELABRA!

BY THE PERSPECTIVE PAINTINGS OF GIOTTO!

BETTER CHECK TO SEE IF ANYTHING WAS STOLEN!

WHY ARE YOU STARING AT ME? IS SOMETHING WRONG?

NO... NO... NOTH- ING...

127

AFTER A QUICK INSPECTION...

EVERYTHING'S HERE, EXCEPT FOR SOME DRAWINGS OF MACHINES.

IF THE THIEF HOPES TO GET AWAY WITH IT, HE'S MAKING A BIG MISTAKE!

I'LL ORDER THE ROYAL GUARDS TO SEARCH THE CASTLES AND THE VILLAGE, HOUSE BY HOUSE!

BONZETON AND I WILL JOIN THE SEARCH, YOUR MAJESTY!

MY FRIENDS AND I WILL, TOO!

NOW, THAT SOUNDS LIKE WORK...

ALL RIGHT, BUT FIRST LET'S CHECK YOUR ROOMS, TOO!

AFTER SEARCHING ALL THE ROOMS WITH NO RESULTS...

WE ALSO LOOKED FOR THE THIEF THROUGH THE STREETS OF AMBOISE...

THAT SAME EVENING, AT THE CASTLE...

NOTHING! WE DIDN'T EVEN FIND A CLUE!

DON'T WORRY, STILTONEAUX, YOU DID WHAT YOU COULD!

WELCOME BACK, CATARD! DO YOU HAVE ANY NEWS?

WE CHECKED THE WOODS, BUT WE DIDN'T FIND ANYTHING!

AND WHERE DID BONZETON WIND UP? DIDN'T YOU GO TOGETHER TO LOOK FOR THE THIEF?

HE AND I GOT SEPARATED. WHO KNOWS WHERE HE WOUND UP?!

THEN WE'LL HAVE TO ORGANIZE A TEAM TO GO SEARCH FOR HIM!

NOT AT ALL! A LITTLE RAIN WILL CLEAR HIS HEAD!

WELL, THAT'S SETTLED! LET'S GO EAT DINNER!

WE HAD DINNER IN SILENCE AND ALMOST NO ONE HAD ANY APPETITE... EXCEPT TRAP!

THEA WAS REALLY WEIRD TODAY...

EVERYTHING'S GOING ACCORDING TO PLAN!

157,563 + 541,027 = 698,590

YUM! THIS CHEESE IS **DELICIOUS!**

THEN WE SET OFF FOR OUR ROOMS...

THERE'S SOMETHING FUNNY ABOUT THIS THEFT!

DO YOU STILL THINK THAT LEONARDO'S TWO ASSISTANTS ARE THE CATS IN DISGUISE?

I DON'T KNOW-- BUT I'M VERY **SUSPICIOUS!**

YET BATTISTA, CATARD AND BONZETON WERE AT THE CHANNEL WITH US!

RIGHT... AND BESIDES, THEY STOLE ALMOST NOTHING!

THAT'S EXACTLY WHAT I CAN'T EXPLAIN!

IT'S TIME TO GO TO SLEEP. MAYBE WE'LL GET SOME IDEAS WHILE WE DREAM!

JUST A MOMENT, THEA! YOU'VE BEEN SO STRANGE LATELY... ARE YOU OKAY?

YES, DON'T WORRY. NOW LET'S ALL GET SOME REST.

HMM... OKAY... *Goodnight!*

GOOD-NIGHT!

'NIGHT!

THREE HOURS LATER...

COUSIN, WOULD YOU STOP WEARING OUT THE FLOOR WITH YOUR PACING?

SORRY.... I'M TOO WORRIED TO SLEEP!

YOU'RE AFRAID YOU WON'T BE ABLE TO STOP THE *PIRATE CATS?*

TO TELL YOU THE TRUTH... I'M WORRIED ABOUT THEA!

WORRIED ABOUT THEA?! WHY?

THIS MORNING, IN LEONARDO'S STUDIO, I FOUND HER NECKLACE ON THE FLOOR!

AND WHAT WAS IT DOING THERE?

THAT'S WHAT I KEEP ASKING MYSELF!

DO YOU SUSPECT THAT SHE STOLE THE DRAWINGS?

NO, BUT... LATELY SHE'S BEEN ACTING STRANGELY!

IN MY OPINION, YOU'RE TIRED AND EXAGGERATING!

MAYBE SHE ENTERED THE STUDIO, SAW THE KING ON THE GROUND, AND BECAUSE SHE WAS AFRAID SHE'D BE BLAMED FOR THE THEFT, RAN AWAY INSTEAD OF SOUNDING THE ALARM!

THAT'S NOT HOW THEA WOULD ACT! AND HOW DO YOU EXPLAIN THE NECKLACE ON THE FLOOR?

I WOULDN'T KNOW... DID YOU ASK HER?

I TRIED TO, BUT BETWEEN ONE THING AND ANOTHER...

:HMPH: I GET IT! IF I WANT TO SLEEP, I'LL HAVE TO GO WITH YOU TO GET HER TO CLEAR THINGS UP!

A FEW MINUTES LATER...

WE HAVE TO BE QUIET. I DON'T WANT TO WAKE UP THE WHOLE CASTLE!

?!?

BUT... WHAT'S THEA DOING?

MAYBE SHE WANTS A SNACK! LET'S FOLLOW HER!

SHE'S KNOCKING ON THE DOOR OF CATARD AND BONZETON'S ROOM!

NOK NOK

I DON'T UNDERSTAND... WHAT'S GOING ON? LOOK, TRAP, COMING OUT OF THE ROOM IS...

...CATARDONE! AND WHY IS THEA WITH HIM? THEY'VE STOPPED IN FRONT OF LEONARDO'S ROOM!

THEY'RE GOING IN!

WHY IS THEA FOLLOWING HIM? AND WHAT ARE THEY LOOKING FOR?

MAYBE THE KEY TO THE KITCHEN, FOR A SNACK!

NOW'S NOT THE TIME FOR JOKING AROUND!

COME ON... LET'S GO IN, TOO!

UMM... MAY I COME IN?

BUT THERE'S NO ONE HERE!

THE WINDOW! IT'S WIDE OPEN!

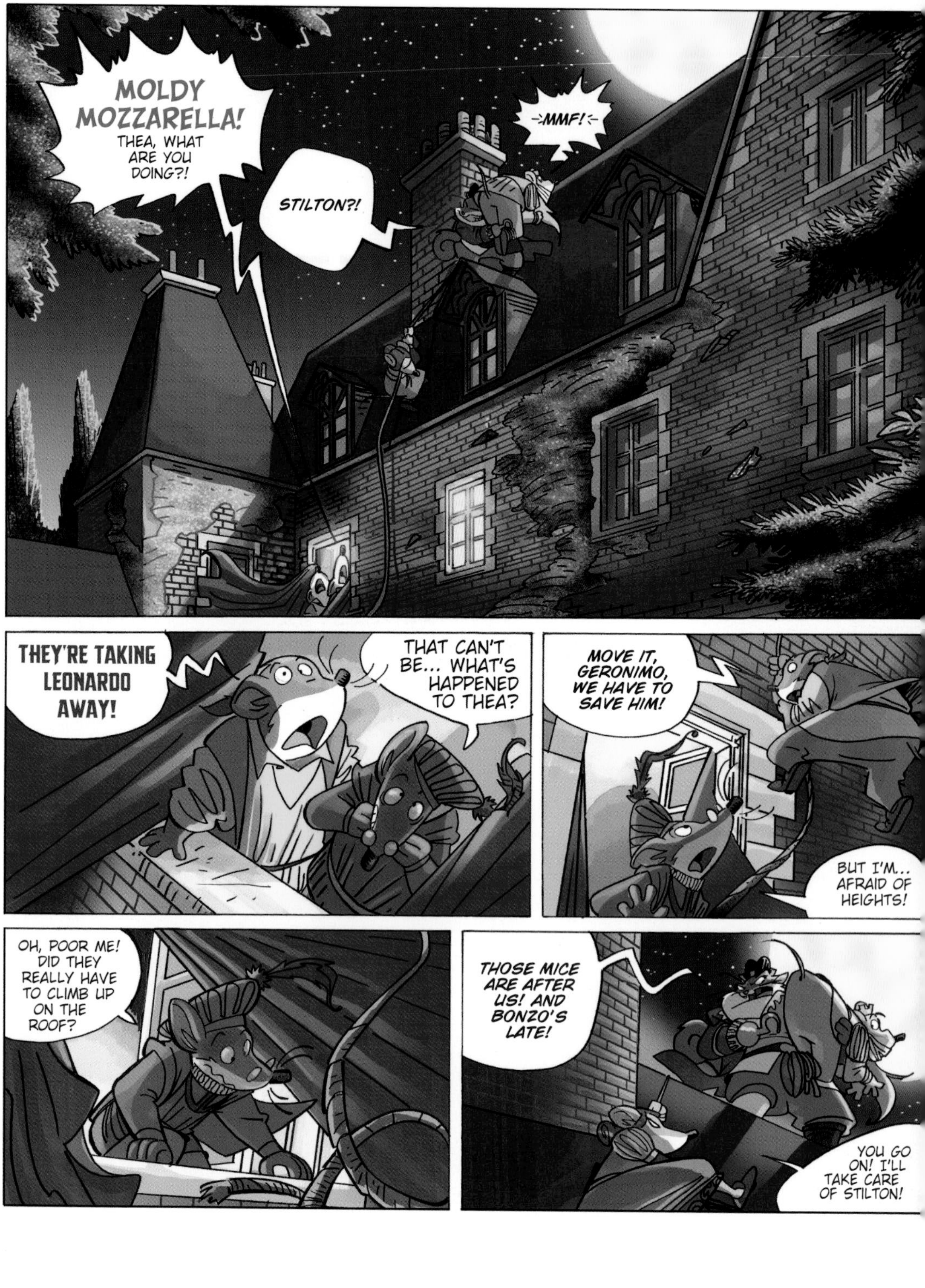
MOLDY MOZZARELLA! THEA, WHAT ARE YOU DOING?!
STILTON?!
-MMF!-
THEY'RE TAKING LEONARDO AWAY!
THAT CAN'T BE... WHAT'S HAPPENED TO THEA?
MOVE IT, GERONIMO, WE HAVE TO SAVE HIM!
BUT I'M... AFRAID OF HEIGHTS!
OH, POOR ME! DID THEY REALLY HAVE TO CLIMB UP ON THE ROOF?
THOSE MICE ARE AFTER US! AND BONZO'S LATE!
YOU GO ON! I'LL TAKE CARE OF STILTON!

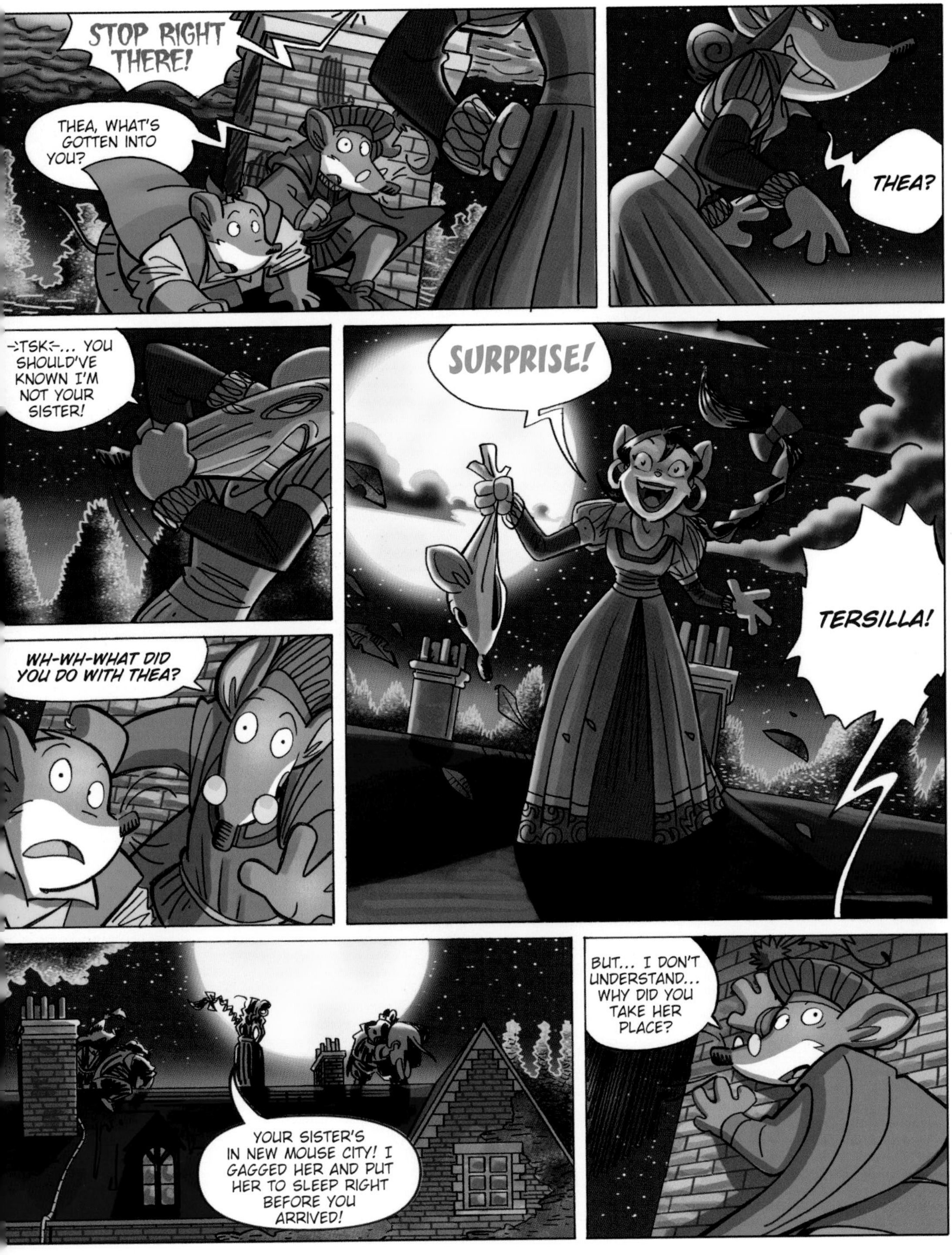
STOP RIGHT THERE!
THEA, WHAT'S GOTTEN INTO YOU?
THEA?
-TSK-... YOU SHOULD'VE KNOWN I'M NOT YOUR SISTER!
SURPRISE!
TERSILLA!
WH-WH-WHAT DID YOU DO WITH THEA?
YOUR SISTER'S IN NEW MOUSE CITY! I GAGGED HER AND PUT HER TO SLEEP RIGHT BEFORE YOU ARRIVED!
BUT... I DON'T UNDERSTAND... WHY DID YOU TAKE HER PLACE?

OBVIOUSLY, TO DISCOVER HOW YOU FIND OUT ABOUT OUR TIME TRAVELS--AND TO KEEP YOU FROM ALWAYS MAKING OUR PLANS GO UP IN SMOKE!

NOW I KNOW ALL ABOUT PROFESSOR VON VOLT AND HIS TEMPO-GRAPH!

YOU CRUMMY CAT! I'M GOING TO MAKE YOU PAY FOR THIS!

SO IT WAS YOU WHO STOLE THE DRAWINGS FROM LEONARDO'S STUDIO AND HIT THE KING!

EXACTLY! I WANTED TO THROW OFF YOUR SUSPICIONS AND MAKE YOU THINK THAT THE CATS HAD COME FROM OUTSIDE! THE BEE GAVE ME AN EXCUSE TO LEAVE AND GO BACK TO THE CASTLE...

"THE INVESTIGATION WOULD HAVE CONTINUED AND WE PIRATE CATS WOULD HAVE BEEN ABLE TO OPERATE WITHOUT BEING DISTURBED... AND KIDNAP LEONARDO!"

"AS FOR THE KING, I DIDN'T EXPECT TO MEET HIM. BUT TAKING CARE OF HIM WAS CHILD'S PLAY!"

I BET YOU BROKE YOUR **NECKLACE** WHEN YOU HIT HIM, AND THAT'S WHY IT WAS ON THE FLOOR!

HUH? IT LOOKS LIKE I MADE A MISTAKE! I WAS IN SUCH A HURRY THAT I DIDN'T EVEN NOTICE I'D LOST IT!

BUT WHY DID YOU WANT TO **KIDNAP** LEONARDO?

TO DECODE THE TEXT ON THIS PARCHMENT! IT MUST HAVE INSTRUCTIONS FOR FINDING A CAT-TAS-TIC TREASURE!

TIME FOR US TO SAY GOODBYE, STILTON: BONZO'S HERE WITH THE CATJET!

HE PRETENDED TO GET LOST IN THE WOODS SO HE COULD GO GET THE TIME MACHINE!

QUICK, GERONIMO... YOU'VE GOT TO DO SOMETHING!

ME? WHAT?

WHATEVER!

→GULP!←

I'M SLIIIIDING!

SQUEEEEE

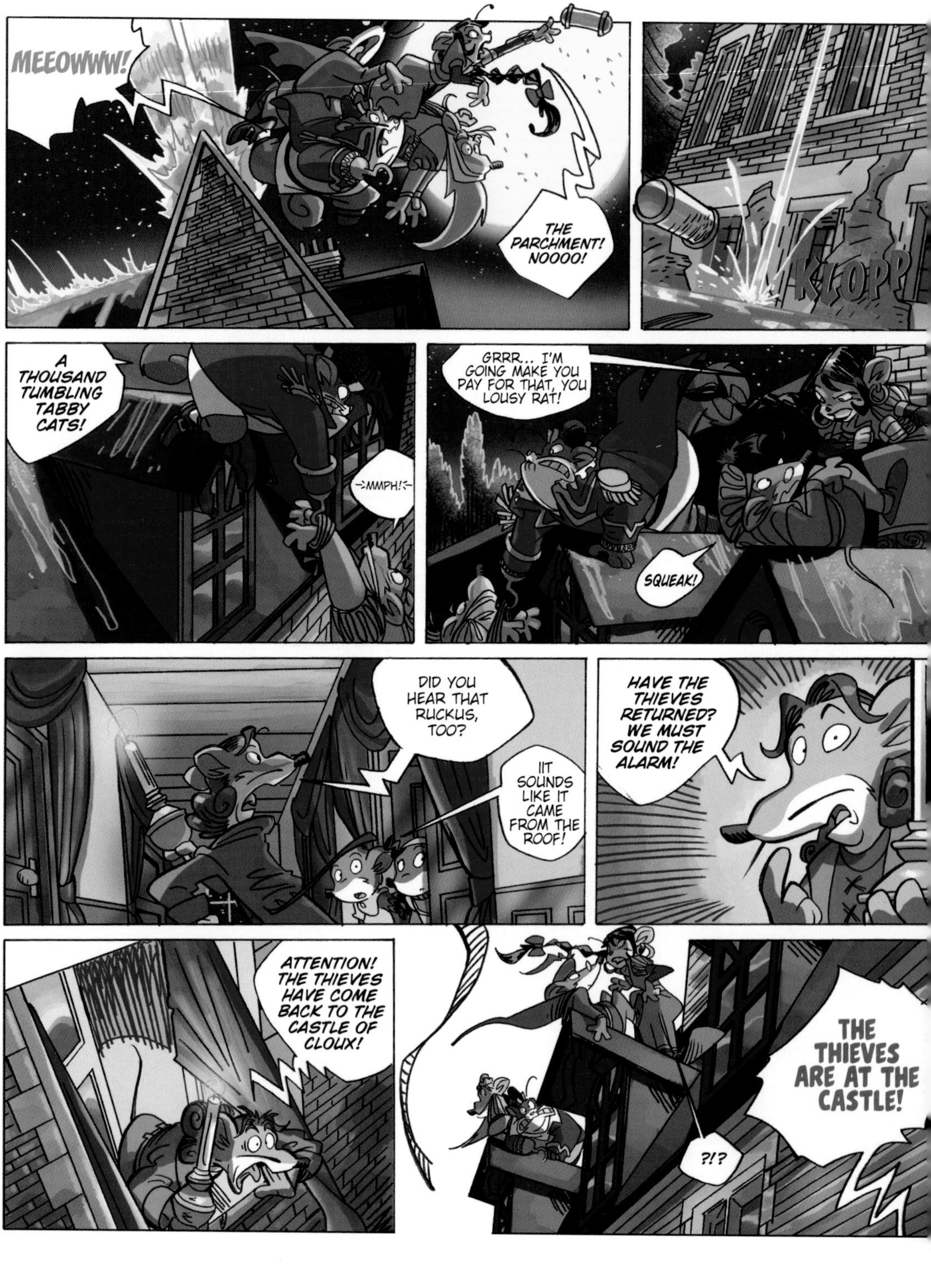

MEEOWWW!
THE PARCHMENT! NOOOO!
KLOPP
A THOUSAND TUMBLING TABBY CATS!
-MMPH!-
GRRR... I'M GOING MAKE YOU PAY FOR THAT, YOU LOUSY RAT!
SQUEAK!
DID YOU HEAR THAT RUCKUS, TOO?
IIT SOUNDS LIKE IT CAME FROM THE ROOF!
HAVE THE THIEVES RETURNED? WE MUST SOUND THE ALARM!
ATTENTION! THE THIEVES HAVE COME BACK TO THE CASTLE OF CLOUX!
?!?
THE THIEVES ARE AT THE CASTLE!

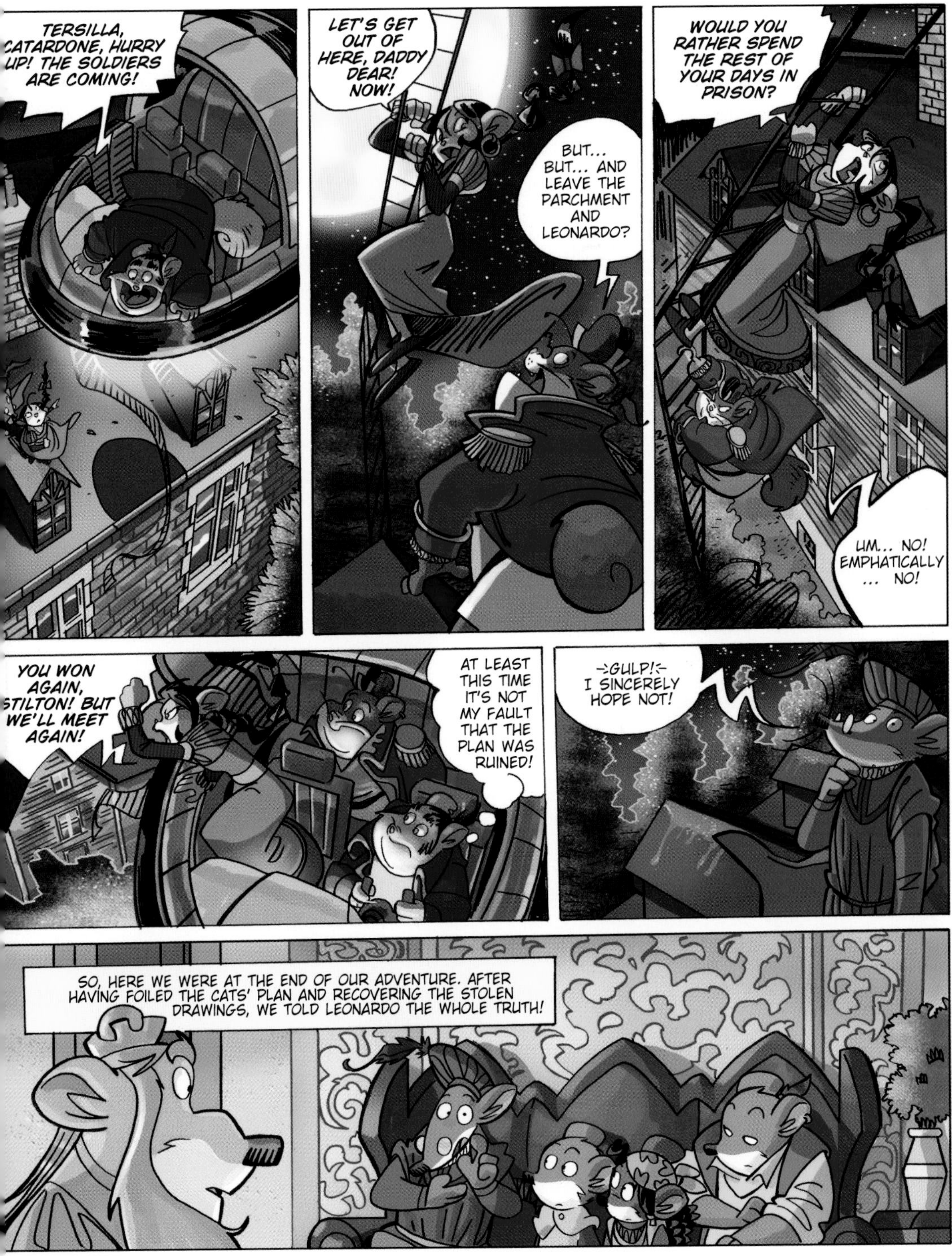

TERSILLA, CATARDONE, HURRY UP! THE SOLDIERS ARE COMING!
LET'S GET OUT OF HERE, DADDY DEAR! NOW!
BUT... BUT... AND LEAVE THE PARCHMENT AND LEONARDO?
WOULD YOU RATHER SPEND THE REST OF YOUR DAYS IN PRISON?
UM... NO! EMPHATICALLY ... NO!
YOU WON AGAIN, STILTON! BUT WE'LL MEET AGAIN!
AT LEAST THIS TIME IT'S NOT MY FAULT THAT THE PLAN WAS RUINED!
GULP! I SINCERELY HOPE NOT!
SO, HERE WE WERE AT THE END OF OUR ADVENTURE. AFTER HAVING FOILED THE CATS' PLAN AND RECOVERING THE STOLEN DRAWINGS, WE TOLD LEONARDO THE WHOLE TRUTH!

WHEN WE TOLD HIM ABOUT THE TIME MACHINE, HE DIDN'T SEEM SURPRISED!

I WAS SURE THERE'D BE TIME TRAVEL SOONER OR LATER!

BUT I WON'T TELL ANYONE ANYTHING ABOUT IT, SO THAT HISTORY DOESN'T CHANGE!

THANK YOU, YOU'RE A TRU *gentlemouse*

BETTER YET, I'D BE CURIOUS TO SEE THE PARCHMENT!

HERE IT IS! IT FELL FROM THE ROOF!

ROLLICKING RATS! IT'S... THE RECIPE FOR RIBOLLITA!

RIBOLLITA?!?

SJCPMMJUB

IT MUST BE A JOKE FROM SOME PRANKSTER COOK! IT'S WRITTEN IN A CODE WHERE EACH LETTER IN A WORD IS WRITTEN DOWN BY USING THE NEXT LETTER IN THE ALPHABET! LOOK, HERE'S THE CODE: R=S, I=J, B=C, O=P, L=M, L=M, I=J, T=U, A=B!

THOSE CATS WENT TO ALL THAT TROUBLE JUST FOR A BOWL OF SOUP?

HA, HA, HA!

IT SEEMS LIKE A VERY GOOD REASON TO ME!

RIBOLLITA

IS A TYPICAL TUSCAN SOUP. ITS INGREDIENTS ARE KALE, BEETS, SAVOY CABBAGE, LEEKS, ONIONS, CELERY, POTATOES, CARROTS, ZUCCHINI, TOMATOES, CANNELLINI BEANS, EXTRA-VIRGIN OLIVE OIL, SALT, PEPPER, AND BREAD. BOIL THE BEANS AND SAUTÉ THE ONIONS AND OTHER CHOPPED VEGETABLES IN THE OLIVE OIL. ADD THE BEANS, HALF OF WHICH HAVE BEEN PUT THROUGH A SIEVE AND THE OTHER HALF LEFT WHOLE. COOK OVER A SLOW FIRE FOR AROUND TWO HOURS. ADD THE SLICED BREAD, SALT, AND PEPPER AND SERVE WITH A DROP OF OLIVE OIL.

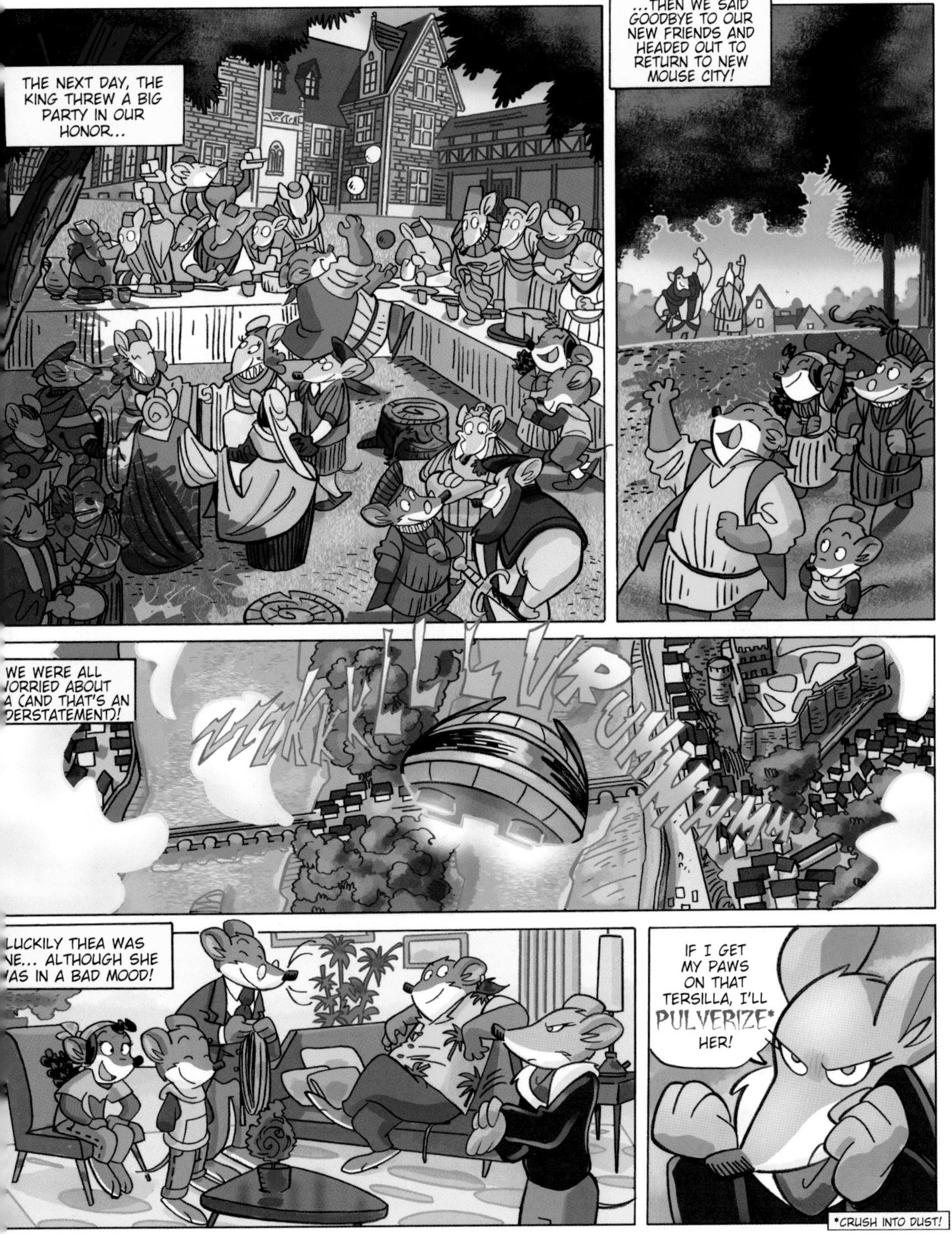

THE NEXT DAY, THE KING THREW A BIG PARTY IN OUR HONOR...
...THEN WE SAID GOODBYE TO OUR NEW FRIENDS AND HEADED OUT TO RETURN TO NEW MOUSE CITY!
WE WERE ALL
ORRIED ABOUT
A (AND THAT'S AN
DERSTATEMENT)!
LUCKILY THEA WAS
NE... ALTHOUGH SHE
AS IN A BAD MOOD!
IF I GET MY PAWS ON THAT TERSILLA, I'LL PULVERIZE* HER!

*CRUSH INTO DUST!

A LITTLE LATER, WE'D MADE OUR WAY BACK TO PROFESSOR VON VOLT'S LAB, AND WE TOLD HIM THE WHOLE STORY...

I'M HAPPY THAT THE MISSION WAS A SUCCESS!

BUT NOW THE PIRATE CATS KNOW ABOUT YOUR LAB AND THE TEMPO-GRAPH!

WELL, MY LABORATORY'S ALWAYS ON THE MOVE, SO THOSE CRUMMY CATS WON'T BE ABLE TO LOCATE IT! AND THEY'RE NOT GOING TO BE ABLE TO TRICK THE *TEMPOGRAPH!*

SO SHALL WE BEGIN OUR *CELEBRATION?*

⇒SLURP!⇐ DEFINITELY!

SO, GERONIMO, WHAT KIND OF A BIRD, OR RATHER A RAT, WAS LEONARDO?

HE WAS LIKE YOU IN MANY WAYS, PROFESSOR!

THANKS FOR THE COMPLIMENT! I'VE ALWAYS CONSIDERED LEONARDO TO BE ONE OF MY TEACHERS! AND I THINK I'VE FOLLOWED HIS TEACHING TO GOOD EFFECT.

⇒TSK⇐... FROM THE LOOK OF THIS DRAWING, I WOULDN'T EXACTLY SAY SO!

⇒GULP!⇐

MY DEAR RODENT FRIENDS, FAREWELL UNTIL THE NEXT ADVENTURE... ANOTHER WHISKERFUL OF AN ADVENTURE, WRITTEN BY STILTON...

Geronimo Stilton!

Watch Out For
PAPERCUT**Z**™

Welcome to the second sci-fi-tinged GERONIMO STILTON 3 IN 1 graphic novel, collecting three great GERONIMO STILTON graphic novels: "Following the Trail of Marco Polo," "The Great Ice Age," and "Who Stole the Mona Lisa?," from Papercutz— those cheese-loving souls dedicated to publishing great graphic novels for all ages. Oh, and I'm Salicrup, *Jim Salicrup*, the Editor-in-Chief and long-time subscriber of The Rodent's Gazette, here to offer a couple of major announcements and to even share a little philosophy with you…

First a little sad news…while we announced "Saving Liberty" in GERONIMO STILTON #19 as the next GERONIMO STILTON graphic novel, alas, that's not to be. For those of you still hoping to enjoy a graphic novel history about the Statue of Liberty may I suggest the hard-to-find "The Gift," by Henry Gibson, writer (he was also a brilliant actor and poet), and Alfredo P. Alcala, artist, published in 1986 by Blackthorne Publishing. Easier to find might be "The Story of the Statue of Liberty," by Xavier W. Niz, writer, and Cynthia Martin, artist, published in 2006 by Capstone Press.

But the good news is that we're publishing a new series entitled GERONIMO STILTON REPORTER! Each volume will be adapting the animated adventures of Geronimo Stilton, and the first volume starts off with the first episode from Season One: "Operation Shufongfong." Unlike the previous GERONIMO STILTON graphic novel series, in which Geronimo and his friends and family would journey back in time to stop the crazy history-altering schemes of the Pirate Cats, GERONIMO STILTON REPORTER is set entirely in the present, as we follow our hero as he covers all sorts of exciting breaking news.

And more good news…if you were paying attention, you saw that we just mentioned the "animated adventures of Geronimo Stilton." In case you hadn't heard, you can now watch Geronimo Stilton on NetFlix! Is that exciting or what?

Finally, we did promise you a little bit of philosophy. As we've done in GERONIMO STILTON #18 and #19, as well as in GERONIMO STILTON REPORTER #1, we're going to share and talk a little about the Philosophy of GERONIMO STILTON, as revealed on geronimostilton.com. This philosophy is more or less the guidelines that are followed by everyone creating GERONIMO STILTON stories, be it for comics, chapter books, or TV. So let's get right to it…

GERONIMO STILTON AND HAPPINESS
Geronimo teaches that real happiness is not wanting what you don't have, but appreciating that which you do have. Attention should be focused on the positive aspects of existence and not on the what is missing. True gratification isn't tied to fleeting and occasional pleasures, but derives from putting your energy towards positive purposes.

As I mentioned in GERONIMO STILTON REPORTER #1, that's EXACTLY my philosophy too. Gee, do all Editor-in-Chiefs think alike? While it's easy for us to say the above, it's another thing to live it. It's part of human (and mouse) nature to want what you can't have. And there's nothing wrong with working to accomplish your goals. But the important point here is to always appreciate what you actually have—whether it's family, friends, or simply someone who has a positive impact on your life.

Speaking of which, we greatly appreciate you! We're thankful that you enjoy GERONIMO STILTON graphic novels because we love publishing them. In fact, we hope you enjoyed GERONIMO STILTON 3 IN 1 #2, and that you'll be back for #3 which features the next three graphic novels: "Dinosaurs in Action," "Play It Again, Mozart!," and "The Weird Book Machine."

See you in the future,

Jim

STAY IN TOUCH!

EMAIL:	salicrup@papercutz.com	INSTAGRAM:	@papercutzgn
WEB:	papercutz.com	FACEBOOK:	PAPERCUTZGRAPHICNOVELS
TWITTER:	@papercutzgn	SNAIL MAIL:	Papercutz, 160 Broadway, Suite 700, East Wing, New York, NY 10038

Thea Stilton

GRAPHIC NOVELS AVAILABLE FROM PAPERCUTZ

...ALSO AVAILABLE WHEREVER E-BOOKS ARE SOLD!

#1
"The Secret
of Whale Island"

#2
"Revenge of
the Lizard Club"

#3
"The Treasure of
the Viking Ship"

#4
"Catching the
Giant Wave"

#5
"The Secret of the
Waterfall in the Woods"

#6
"The Thea Sisters and
the Myster at Sea"

#7
"A Song for the
Thea Sisters"

papercutz.com